A horseman had suddenly appeared.

In the distance th[...] [...] where Jessie and [...] [...] dark figure silhou[...] [...] sky. All that they could tell about him was that he wore a broad-brimmed hat and a long, cloaklike coat or duster that fell in folds almost to his stirrups.

"There doesn't seem to be anybody with him," Ki said. "But you might be right, Jessie. Maybe he's the man who—"

Ki broke off as another ragged volley of shots came from the rustlers on the slope of the mesa. At the rim of the mesa the strange rider had dismounted and was shedding his long duster. He tossed it across his saddle and started down the sloping side. As he moved, he was drawing pistols from the holsters that were now visible low on each hip. He moved with long strides, jumping rather than running, as he angled across the slanting face of the wide mesa.

Puffs of powdersmoke began spurting from the mesa's face, and tiny dust-clouds rose from the ground on both sides of the lone shootist as the rustlers began to return his fire. The stranger did not interrupt his zigzag advance.

"I don't know who that man is, Jessie, but he's certainly not one of the rustlers!"

WESLEY ELLIS
LONE STAR

AND THE
JAMES GANG'S LOOT

J

JOVE BOOKS, NEW YORK

LONE STAR AND THE JAMES GANG'S LOOT

A Jove Book/published by arrangement with
the author

PRINTING HISTORY
Jove edition/January 1988

ISBN: 0-515-09379-3

Jove Books are published by The Berkley Publishing Group,
200 Madison Avenue, New York, New York 10016.
The name "JOVE" and the "J" logo
are trademarks belonging to Jove Publications, Inc.

PRINTED IN THE UNITED STATES OF AMERICA

10 9 8 7 6 5 4 3 2 1

Chapter 1

"I was really surprised to see you again, Joe, after all these years," Jessie said to the army officer at her right.

She was sitting at the head of the long table in the big dining room of the Circle Star. The officer she'd addressed as Joe was wearing dress blues with the gold leaf insignia of a major on the shoulders of his jacket. He sat across the table from Ki, who'd just returned to his seat after clearing away their dessert plates and filling coffee-cups for Jessie and the officer and pouring himself tea from the pot that rested on a serving-table behind him.

"But you were just a lieutenant then," Jessie went on. "I see you've moved along pretty quickly."

"Probably faster than I deserved," Major Farnum answered, "but I've been lucky."

When she and Farnum had met for the first time, he'd been out of West Point for only a few years, newly stationed at Fort Chaplin on the Texas-Mexico border. Jessie and Ki had been chasing a small band of rustlers who were pushing cattle they'd stolen from the Circle Star toward the Rio Grande.

In the perennially man-short army, Farnum had been the only man free to give them the assistance they'd requested

1

from the fort's commandant. When the rustlers had split their stolen herd in an effort to confuse their pursuers, Ki had followed one bunch while Jessie and Farnum trailed the second. In the shooting that had followed when they caught up with the small band, Farnum had gotten a bullet crease in one arm. While they rested in a secluded canyon by the Rio Grande, they'd become lovers.

"I'm just happy that you remembered me and welcomed me at your ranch after I'd waited such a long time to accept your invitation to visit," the major replied.

Jessie nodded. "It has been a while, at that. But I'm glad you decided to stop on the way to your new assignment."

"By the time I'd gotten to Texas from Washington, I'd recovered from my surprise at being posted to Fort Chaplin again, after such a long time," Major Farnum told her. "I could hardly believe it when I got the order to reactivate the fort. But with the troubles that're developing so fast on the other side of the Rio Grande, I suppose it was a wise decision."

"It'll be almost like going home, won't it?" Ki asked.

"In a way it will." Farnum nodded. "But the army had become my real home even before my father died."

Jessie's only reply was a nod. She had learned earlier, at the time when she'd first met Farnum, that the army officer had never known of his father's ties to the vicious international cartel whose hired killers had murdered Alex Starbuck. The young army officer had not been aware of the years which Jessie and Ki had devoted to smashing the cartel. Most importantly, he'd never learned that the elder Farnum had been among the several prominent industrialists whom the cartel's bosses had ordered murdered during one of the group's internal struggles over leadership.

Ki took advantage of the momentary silence to say

2

"Please excuse me, if you will. Since this is gathers-time, we're shorthanded here at the main house, and I have a few things to attend to before bedtime."

"Of course." Jessie nodded. "You don't need to break your routine because of our guest, Ki. I'll show him to his room."

"Well, I'm glad you'll get a chance to see the Circle Star at last," Jessie said later, breaking the silence that had fallen between them after Farnum's remark about his father's death and Ki's departure. "I remember on our first meeting how surprised you were when you learned the size of some of the spreads here in Texas. Now, I'll have a chance to show you how important rangeland is to all the ranches in this part of the country."

"I'm afraid I won't have time to look at your ranch as closely as I'd like to, Jessie," Farnum told her. "You see, I'm really here on time I'm stealing from the army."

"That sounds terrible!" Jessie smiled. "I hope there's no danger that you'll be court-martialed for going a few miles out of your way."

"I'll admit I'm just trying to impress you," Farnum said. His smile matched Jessie's. "But quite seriously, I won't have time for more than a quick look at your ranch. Right at this minute there's a detachment of infantry on the way to my new station from Fort Sam Houston, and two cavalry troops riding down from Fort Bliss, and I've got to be at my post in time to meet them. Besides, I didn't come to look at your ranch or cattle. I came to see you."

"And?" Jessie smiled.

"And you're the same fascinating woman I've remembered since our first meeting. The most honest one, too. You told me the truth when you said there wasn't room for marriage in your life. I've learned a bit about your father

3

while I was learning about the responsibilities you inherited."

"Now you're flattering me too much," Jessie told him. "But you'll have to see some of the Circle Star in spite of yourself. You've ridden over part of it on the way to the house, and you'll be riding over more on your way to the fort."

"I was hoping you'd ride part of the way with me, but from what Ki said this is a busy time for you." A small frown formed on his face. "Tell me, Jessie, what the devil are gathers?"

"You know we run a sizable number of cattle on the Circle Star," Jessie replied. "If all the steers were in one big herd, there wouldn't be enough grass or water for them. So we separate them into several herds on different parts of our range. When we start getting our marked herd together, the hands go in pairs to cut out the marketable steers from those scattered herds and gather them into one herd that'll be shipped to market."

"That's what you're doing now?"

Jessie nodded. "Yes. Ki and I are almost alone here at the main house during the gathers."

"You know what this reminds me of, don't you, Jessie?"

"I think so. It's pretty much like the first time we were together, in that canyon on the border," she said. "When Ki had gone scouting and left us there alone."

"I've never forgotten those few days we had," Farnum told her, his voice husky.

She nodded. "Neither have I. And if you're wondering whether we can recapture them, since you rode up to the house I've been wondering the same thing."

Standing up, Jessie extended her hand. Farnum grasped it and followed her as they passed through the study, which had been her father's favorite room, along the short hall-

4

way beyond it and up the stairs. Halfway down the dim corridor a door stood ajar, lamplight spilling from it. Through the half-open door, Farnum could see a wide roomy bed, an armchair, and a lamp burning on a small bedside table.

"It's a lot more comfortable than the hard riverbank in the canyon," Jessie said as she took his hand and led him inside. "But we'll be just as much alone."

Farnum wasted no words. He embraced Jessie and she turned her face up for his kiss. For a moment after they broke their embrace they stood hesitantly in the fashion of lovers who have been parted for a long time and meet almost as strangers. Then Jessie stepped up to the lamp and blew it out.

Blind in the darkness, they let their fingers guide them as they helped one another to undress. Then as familiarity was restored by the touch of their hands and by the kisses they exchanged as they helped each other to undress, all was well, and there was no longer any strangeness between them.

Jessie woke in the grey dimness of first dawn to find Farnum propped up on one elbow, looking at her. She smiled up at him.

"Sometimes I forget that ranching isn't the only kind of life that encourages waking up early," she said.

"No. If I was on duty, I'd be up getting ready to order the bugler to sound morning parade," he replied. "But I'd much rather be here with you. For the last few minutes I've been looking at you and wondering how soon I'd dare to wake you up. And watching you sleep is a pleasure I've been thinking about ever since I decided to stop and visit you."

"Would you like for me to close my eyes again?"

"If you don't object to playing games at this hour of the morning."

Jessie closed her eyes. In a moment she felt the soft pressure of Farnum's lips on her cheek, passing over her flawless silken skin with the gentle pressure of a butterfly's wings. He touched his lips to her closed eyelids, then slowly trailed them down to the hollows of her throat and moved on to the yet-unbudded rosettes of her swelling breasts.

Though she did not open her eyes, Jessie was increasingly aware of the progress of Farnum's questing lips. He found the pebbling tips of her generous breasts and began caressing them softly. Jessie lay quietly, enjoying the sensations that were beginning to ripple through her body. The memory of the night was still strong, and gave her a vivid picture of what still lay ahead.

As she began responding more fully to the pleasure of the soft caresses she was receiving, Jessie's hand slid down to her lover's groin. She began responding to his attentions, closing her hand on his swelling shaft, tightening, then relaxing the pressure of her fingers with a steadily more urgent rhythm.

By now the grayness of the pre-sunrise dawn was creeping into the room. Jessie could make out her lover's features, and the sight of Farnum's chisel-featured tanned face moving from side to side as he caressed one of her budded tips for a few moments before transferring his attention to its twin, increased the pleasure that was taking over her body.

As her sensations mounted, Farnum's throbbing, swelling flesh told her that he was as ready as she was. Jessie whispered, "I don't want to wait any longer, and you're as ready as I am. Come into me now."

Farnum needed no second invitation. As Jessie opened

her thighs to receive him, he rose above her and she sighed with delight as he drove into her with his engorged shaft. Farnum began thrusting, and Jessie responded. Their rhythm started slowly, deliberately, and then mounted steadily.

A moan formed deep in Jessie's throat. She released it as a soft sigh of pleasure as Farnum kept plunging. His stroking grew steadily faster until she started to tremble. When her slow tremors intensified, Jessie clasped her arms around Farnum and locked her ankles around his back to draw him into her still more deeply.

Although her first responses had been measured and slow, as the minutes ticked off they mounted into frantic writhing heaves which soon became a spasmic, frantic frenzy. Then Farnum's steady stroking became fierce downward lunges, increasing in speed and intensity as each moment passed. Finally he lunged, driving deeply as his own peak approached, until at last he plunged into her with a last deep stroke and held himself against her quivering body.

For several minutes Jessie had been moaning with little happy sighs. When she felt Farnum lunge in his last spasmic thrust she cried out in ecstasy and locked her arms around him as though to make their bodies one. When he fell on her heavily after she took him across the threshold into a shared ecstasy, Jessie held him even closer. Her cries faded as Farnum's quivering gradually diminished after his own final spasm. She was quiet then, holding him clasped close against her while the tremors that were shaking both of them subsided. They lay quietly, still in a close embrace.

Rays of pink sunrise were creeping into the room around the drawn window-shade when Jessie stirred again. She said, "I don't really want to say this, but we've both got responsibilities to think about."

"I'm afraid you're right," he agreed. Bending to kiss her, Farnum got up and started dressing.

As he raised his hand to slide into his gray flannel army shirt, Jessie noticed a wealed scar on his arm. Interrupting her dressing, she remarked, "That bullet wound you got when we were chasing those rustlers seems to have healed very nicely."

"Thanks to the care you gave me then, it has. And not that I needed one, but it's a constant reminder of you, Jessie."

"Now that you know the way to the Circle Star, you'll have to come visit me often."

"I'd like nothing better, but we've got to get the border peaceful again. After that—who knows? I might be transferred back to one of the eastern forts again."

"Be sure to let me know," Jessie told him, "because from time to time I travel east on business. Now, let's go down to breakfast. I'm sure Ki has it ready, and I don't know about you, but I'm starving."

Ki did indeed have breakfast ready. Jessie and Farnum ate slowly, brushing hands now and then, smiling at one another across the table, until the last strip of bacon was gone and the platter of flapjacks emptied.

"I'm afraid I've run out of excuses for staying, Jessie," he said, regret shading his voice. "I'm going to have to saddle up and ride."

Ki had come into the dining room in time to hear Farnum's remark. He said, "You won't have to bother about saddling, Major," he said. "I had one of our hands do that while you and Jessie were eating."

"That was very thoughtful, Ki," Farnum said. "Thank you." He turned to Jessie and went on, "Until the next time, then. And if you ever get close to the fort, I'll be very disappointed if you pass by without stopping."

With a half-salute, Farnum turned and went out. Jessie said to Ki, "It's time we were getting busy, too. There's that little herd of scrubs that the hands have choused into the east section. I'd like to take another look at them, just to be sure there aren't a few more head that will make the market herd. And after that, we've got the northwest range to inspect, to see what the men brought in from the north section yesterday."

"I thought you might want to be out on the range," Ki told her. "So I had Sun saddled after the major's horse was ready. We can ride whenever you want to."

"We'll make an easy day of it," Jessie said. "Ride the northwest section first, then swing back by the house in time to eat at noon. We can finish the day with a look at the scrubs."

Still smiling now and then as she recalled some fleeting moment of the night and morning that she'd spent in the arms of her lover, Jessie saw the fence ahead and reined Sun. Letting the magnificent palomino move ahead slowly she brought him to a halt as it came within a yard or so of the seemingly endless strands of barbwire that marked the beginning of the Circle Star's northwest range. Ki had been letting Jessie take the lead. He rode up abreast of Sun now, pulled up, and pointed to the straggled-out little herd of steers that grazed lazily beyond the fence.

"This is just one bunch," he said. "The rest are pretty well scattered out. But if you want to take a closer look at what's here, we can ride down to the gate. It's only about a half-mile, and still early."

Jessie had been inspecting the cattle on the other side of

9

the fence. Without taking her eyes off the steers, she shook her head.

"I don't think we need to, Ki," she said. "From the way this herd looks, and its size, we're getting fewer scrubs this year than we ever have before."

"I've noticed that, too," he nodded. "All those years that Alex, and now you, have been checking the breeding bulls are paying off in better stock."

"We don't really have enough scrubs this year to bother sending them to market," Jessie went on. "After market, I think the best thing to do is have the men drive them over to that small southeast section and carry them over the winter."

"Whatever you say," Ki agreed. "I'll tell—" He broke off as the thudding distant hoofbeats of a galloping horse reached their ears.

Jessie heard the pounding rhythm at the same time and turned also. A little frown creased her forehead under the wide brim of her tobacco-hued, Plains-creased Stetson as she said, "That's Manny Esquivel's pony, Ki. And he's coming for us in a hurry. Where was he supposed to be working today?"

"He left right after breakfast to make tally on the southeast range, Jessie. The men have been loading it pretty heavily and I needed to get some idea how to distribute the other steers that'll be coming in."

"Manny's not one of our hurry-up hands," Jessie said. "It must be something important, or he wouldn't've come looking for us in the first place."

"He's cutting leather, all right," Ki agreed.

They sat in silence, watching the rider draw closer, until he reined in beside them.

"What's happened, Manny?" Jessie asked.

"Trouble, Mees Jessie," the ranch-hand replied. "I am

wake up from leetle *siesta* after I eat at noon. Then I see riders. I theenk I go to find out who they are, but they start eshoot at me when they see me."

"You didn't get hit, I hope." Jessie frowned, looking at the man more closely.

"No, no, Mees Jessie. They are too far to eshoot good. But I do not estay; there are many of them and only me to be against them."

"How many were there?" Ki asked.

"Seéx, maybe seven. Ees not close and they move fast. And *los ganados* ees raise so much dust I am not esure of what I am esee."

"Is that all you can tell us?" Jessie asked. Her frown had grown deeper.

"Oh, no, Mees Jessie. Ees more. They esee me ride off, but they do not chase me. They begin round up herd."

"Rustlers!" Jessie exclaimed.

"*Sí,*" Manny agreed. "*Ladrones*. They estart the herd away."

"Did you stay long enough to see which direction they took?" Jessie asked.

"*Seguro,* Mees Jessie. They are go *al sur,* toward border."

"They're heading for Mexico, then," Ki frowned.

"*Seguro que sí,* Ki," Manny nodded.

Turning to Jessie, Ki went on, "That southeast range is where we've been grazing the best of the market cattle, Jessie. If you'll remember, it was your idea to bunch the prime steers together to make tallying easier."

"Yes. But don't you suppose the rustlers probably just picked that southeast range to raid because it was the first one they came to? Not that it matters a great deal," Jessie went on. "We'll go after them, of course, Ki."

"Of course," Ki agreed without hesitation. "I can get to

11

where Ed's working in a hurry, and have him get some of the men together, and—"

Jessie broke in quickly. "No, Ki. Ed's a good foreman, but he's not a fighter. And the hands are too badly scattered. Even if it is only the middle of the afternoon now, it'd take the rest of the day to get even two or three more together, and it'd put too much of a load on the men we'd have to leave behind."

"We'll go after them by ourselves, then?"

"It wouldn't be the first time we've been outnumbered." Jessie smiled. "Besides, we've been idle too long. I don't intend to let Circle Star stock be stolen! Come on. We'll stop at the house to get what we'll need. Then we'll ride on after the rustlers and get those steers back."

Chapter 2

"If we run across a stream or even a mossed-up waterhole in the next half-hour, we'd better stop for the night, Jessie," Ki suggested. "It's getting on for sunset now."

"I was about to say the same thing," Jessie told him. "We haven't been pushing the horses too hard, but they're already lagging a little bit. I'm sure they're thirsty, and even Sun is beginning to show signs of getting tired."

"Of course, the rustlers' horses are getting as tired as ours are," Ki reminded her.

"That doesn't change the odds a bit, Ki," Jessie replied. "Unless they brought along spare horses, we know now that there are eight of them. We're going to need every bit of edge we can get when we catch up with them."

Jessie spoke casually, as though facing a showdown battle against heavy odds was a normal activity. For her and Ki it was, of course. During the long years when they'd been battling the sinister European cartel which had hired the killers who murdered Alex Starbuck, they'd faced even heavier odds than the six-to-one fight they were now sure lay ahead of them.

Throughout those years, Ki had stood by Jessie as faithfully as he'd served her father. It had been Alex Starbuck who'd brought Ki to the United States in the days when Alex had just begun to establish himself as one of the nation's foremost industrial giants. Son of an American father who'd been one of Alex Starbuck's close friends, and a Japanese mother who'd died giving him birth, Ki's samurai grandparents had refused to acknowledge him as a member of their family because of his mixed blood.

In a country as strongly devoted to ancestry and family as Japan, Ki had for all practical purposes become an outcast in his native land. There was only one choice he could make—to become a soldier of fortune. To prepare himself, Ki had spent his early youth moving around the Orient, going from the *dojo* of one martial-arts master to another until his skill in combat was second to none. Encountering Alex by chance, he'd accepted the invitation his father's old friend had given him, and had come with Alex to the United States.

Following Alex's murder, Ki had transferred his loyalty to Jessie. After their destruction of the cartel, he'd remained at the Circle Star, acting as Jessie's good right hand in helping her to operate the vast industrial empire which had been her bequest from her father. Although the job of destroying the cartel had finally been finished, Ki still remained with Jessie, acting as a sort of majordomo in the supervision of the many enterprises that had been her inheritance.

Though the Starbuck industrial empire had many major offices in America's large cities, Jessie had followed her dead father's example in making her own headquarters at the Circle Star, the vast Southwest Texas cattle ranch that had been Alex's haven. To her as well as to Ki, the Circle Star was home, the home Alex Starbuck had created before his untimely death.

Now, though the cattle herd stolen by the rustlers would

not have represented a serious money loss, the idea of rustlers invading their Circle Star range handed a challenge to both Jessie and Ki. Their home had been violated; their objective was to recover the rustled cattle. Their motives had another aspect: they wanted to prove once again that Starbuck property was inviolable.

"We've faced worse odds," Ki pointed out. His voice was almost casual as he went on: "We won't have any trouble picking up the trail in the morning. And I imagine that about this time the rustlers will be holing up for the night, so we won't be giving them any more of a start than they've got now."

"I'm sure they know the country better than we do, though," Jessie said, thinking aloud. "And we'd better assume that they'll be smart enough to stop in a spot where we wouldn't notice them even if we passed close to it. Besides, when I get this far south of the Circle Star, I don't know the landmarks very well."

"That's easy to understand." Ki nodded. "It's been a long time since we rode from the Circle Star to the Rio Grande. And we've followed a lot of strange trails in a lot of different places since we headed for the border the last time."

"From the angle the trail's holding with the sun right now, I'd say the rustlers are heading for that big deserted stretch between Piedras Negras and Nuevo Laredo." Jessie frowned.

Ki nodded. "It wouldn't surprise me. That's the area they favor. Too much land and too few *Rurales* to patrol it. It's always been the place outlaws favor, even if there isn't much water along it."

"They're a good half-day or more ahead of us," Jessie went on. "And I suppose they're making the best time they can. But suppose we were to keep moving, Ki. Wouldn't we have a good chance of catching up with them if we changed the plans we were making a few minutes ago, and rode all night?"

"Yes, I'm sure we would."

"Of course, there's always the chance that we might pass them in the dark and get ahead of them," Jessie went on.

"You know, Jessie, it might be to our advantage if we did just exactly that," Ki suggested. Then, speaking slowly and thoughtfully, he went on: "I'm sure they'll guess we're following them, so they'll be looking for us to come up on them from behind. It'd give us a very good edge if we did pass them in the dark and let them run into us tomorrow."

"And we certainly need every bit of edge we can get," Jessie said.

"We don't have to worry about our horses," Ki went on. "We can be pretty sure ours are in better shape than the nags the rustlers are riding."

"Then let's decide right now," Jessie suggested.

"I say we keep riding," Ki told her.

She nodded. "It makes more sense than stopping. If we come across a waterhole or creek any time soon, we'll stop just long enough to eat a bite and rest the horses; then we'll push on."

Dawn found Jessie and Ki still moving slowly, riding southwest toward the border. At some time during the long hours of steady riding, both of them had passed the strange threshold when sleepiness gives way to wakefulness, and in spite of the long hours they'd been in the saddle, they no longer felt drawn and dragged-out, but almost fresh.

They'd found water just as the sun was beginning to set, and they rested while they ate and let the horses stand idle. Without any further discussion then, they'd ridden ahead,

16

moving slowly but steadily, keeping to the trail by the scant light of the stars and the rising three-quarter moon that soon turned the barren land into a moonscape.

There was almost no vegetation on the stone-hard ground, and the trail left by the stolen herd was marked plainly by the dung piles of the steers and the few areas of relatively soft soil that had been churned up by their hooves. Such soft spots in the baked, barren soil did not occur often, and they'd ridden a substantial distance in the growing dawnlight when Jessie suddenly reined in. Ki pulled up and stopped beside her.

"Is something wrong?" he asked.

"No. But I just realized that we must've lost the trail. I haven't seen a single sign for the past three or four miles that the cattle have passed along here."

"Perhaps they haven't," Ki suggested. "We may be ahead of the herd now. I don't imagine the rustlers would've camped for the night right beside the trail."

"Of course not!" Jessie agreed. "And they certainly wouldn't've lighted a fire to give away their location. But just the same, it might be a good idea for us to separate and ride zigzags on each side of the trail. Dim as it is now and then, we'll just have to assume the rustlers must be following it."

"We're agreed on that, and I'll agree that your idea of scouting on both sides is a good one. But let's be sure to keep one another in sight, Jessie. We've got little enough firepower between us as it is."

"Yes, we'll have to be careful not to lose sight of one another." Jessie nodded. "And if there's any surprising to be done, we'd better be the ones to do it."

With the casual confidence that had grown up between them in the course of many encounters with vicious enemies, Jessie and Ki reined their mounts on diverging

17

courses. As they slanted apart, Jessie rode to the right and Ki to the left. When there was almost a mile between them, Jessie raised her arm and gestured, and even in the distance she could see Ki nodding that he'd understood her meaning. They turned their horses to parallel courses, one of them on each side of the trail, and set out to close in on the rustlers.

They were still following the faint trail, which meandered between them. The sun had risen now, and its low-slanting rays cast their elongated shadows ahead of them. In the brighter light of early morning they could now see the trail more clearly. The brightening rays of the sunlight emphasized the clods of disturbed earth as well as the small hollows of hoofprints that marked the passage of both horses and cattle.

The sun rose still higher and dispelled the ground-shadows that pooled along the trail. They'd covered a mile or so in the fullness of daylight when Jessie began to worry. She pulled Sun to a halt, stood up in her stirrups, and waved for Ki to join her on the trail once more.

"I'm beginning to wonder if we did the right thing, Ki," she told him. "We didn't see any sign during the night that the rustlers had turned off, but there certainly aren't any hoofprints or any other indication that the herd has passed this way."

Ki frowned. "It'd have been very easy to miss seeing the tracks in the dark if they did turn off. And they might've turned and headed straight for the Rio Grande, of course."

"Then we'd better start backtracking," Jessie said decisively. "If they did turn the herd off to bed down for a while, I'm sure they won't be expecting us to meet them head-on."

18

"And in daylight we'll be able to see where they turned the herd off the trail, if that's what they did," Ki agreed.

Turning their horses, Jessie and Ki began retracing the ground they'd already covered. They'd ridden only a half-hour when the strong rays of the climbing sun showed them the tracks they'd missed seeing in the dark. The tracks turned west at right angles to the road and led to a stretch of country broken by the rising humps of low buttes that rose from the sun-parched landscape.

Winding between the buttes there was a line that stretched into the distance, a confusion of hoofprints in which the shod hooves of several horses and the flat V-cleft marks left by the steers intermingled. It marked the spot where the rustlers had left the trail to the south and moved the stolen herd due west.

"They've got a start on us," Jessie told Ki as they leaned forward in their saddles to examine the tracks.

"Two or three hours, I'd guess." Ki nodded. "And they're moving toward the Rio Grande, so they've got a drive of one full day and part of another. We'll catch up with them before they can get to the river."

"Yes," Jessie agreed. "We'll be moving a lot faster than they can. And if we're careful, we'll take them by surprise."

No more words were needed. Jessie and Ki toed their horses ahead and started along beside the welter of intermingled cattle and horse tracks.

By the time Jessie and Ki got their first glimpse of the herd the sun was high in the sky, moving toward its zenith. In the distance the first sign they saw was a little hazy dust-cloud that marked the passage of the steers and the men who'd stolen them. The thin yellowish blotch rose against the cloudless blue sky and hung for minutes before dissolving, but as they drew closer they could see the men on horseback who were riding drag, behind the straggling steers.

Moments later, as they continued to close the gap that separated them from the herd, the flankers who were strung out on either side of the strung-out herd came into sight. Then, in front of the cattle, the bobbing sombreros of the point riders in front of the herd became visible. The trail they were on now led through a maze of small buttes. Like an earthen forest, the buttes dotted the land on each side of the track. Some were bigger than a house; others were only a few feet wide.

Jessie resisted the temptation to spur ahead and start the fight she knew would be necessary to regain the rustled animals. Instead of spurring, she reined in. Ki stopped beside her.

"We'd better split up here," she said. "There's no chance we'll lose sight of them now. We can use the buttes for cover."

Ki nodded. "Take them on both flanks. I'll use my rifle until I get close enough to change to my *shuriken*."

No other planning was required between them. Veterans of many danger-filled encounters, Jessie and Ki were accustomed to working as a team. Ki reined his horse to his left and crossed the trail left by the cattle-thieves and their stolen herd. Jessie waited until Ki turned his mount and started riding parallel to the trail. Then she touched Sun's flank lightly with the toe of one boot and the stallion began moving ahead.

Jessie and Ki could see each other only occasionally now, but those quick glimpses were all they needed as they dodged in and out among the buttes that bordered the beaten trail. They were closing in on the rustler band. Ahead of them, Jessie soon heard lowing coming now and then from one of the steers in the herd. A few moments later the thudding of cattle hooves reached her ears, and occasionally a shout from one of the rustlers as he called to a companion.

Jessie touched Sun's reins lightly, and the big palomino slowed his pace. She looked for Ki, but he was hidden behind one of the buttes on the opposite side of the herd. The dull thuds of hoofbeats were louder now; so were the cattle-blats and calls from the rustlers.

Glancing ahead, Jessie studied the lay of the land. What she saw brought a worried frown to her forehead. A wide expanse of clear ground stretched ahead beyond the buttes. The strip of barren land was less than a quarter of a mile distant. Beyond it the land was barren for another half-mile; then it sloped upward to become the side of a high, wide mesa that filled the horizon as far as she could see on either side. Except for small scattered stands of low-growing dwarf cedars and clumps of even lower-growing prickly pear, the sloping side of the mesa was barren. Its only feature was a narrow zigzag trail leading to its top.

Jessie needed no second look to realize that she and Ki must attack instantly if they were to have any chance at all. Once the rustlers left the area broken by the small buttes, they would see her and Ki almost instantly.

Even though she'd had no chance to study her immediate surroundings, Jessie acted. Prodding Sun's flank with her boot-toe, she dropped the reins to Sun's shoulders and whipped her rifle out of its saddle scabbard. As soon as the weapon was in her grasp, she brought both heels back to touch the palomino's flanks.

Sun knew at once what was expected of him. He lunged ahead and rounded the base of the little butte which had hidden him and Jessie. Ki was nowhere in sight, but Jessie knew that she could count on his being close by. Ahead, the rustled herd was still making its slow but steady progress between the buttes. She saw that four rustlers were strung out on each side along the sides of the herd as flankers. Two more were riding ahead as guides, and the remaining pair rode drag, behind the herd, keeping the cattle from stringing out.

Only seconds after she'd emerged from the shelter of the buttes, Jessie glimpsed Ki as he rode between two small buttes a short distance from the moving herd. He was too far away for Jessie to call to him. She brought up her rifle and leveled it, sighting at the rearmost flanker, aiming low, intending to wound rather than kill.

Before she could find her point of aim, one of the men riding drag turned to look behind him and saw Jessie. He whipped his revolver from its holster and twisted in his saddle. Jessie caught his motion from the corner of her eye, and fired without aiming.

Her shot was low. The rifle's slug struck the rustler's calf and carried through it to lodge in the side of his horse. The wounded animal screamed the shrill hair-raising sound—part neigh, part snort—of a horse that has been hurt. The rustler had been bringing up his pistol when Jessie fired. He got off his shot, but he was already shaking in pain from the rifle slug that had plowed through his leg, and the pistol bullet kicked up a harmless spurt of dust from the ground beside Sun.

Before the cattle-thief who'd fired at Jessie could trigger his revolver a second time, the high, sharp bark of Ki's rifle broke the air, and the man toppled from his saddle and landed on the hard tan earth in the ungainly sprawl of death. The man beside him had pulled his rifle from its saddle scabbard by now. He was raising it, leveling it at Jessie, when the second shot from her Winchester knocked him from his horse.

22

Ki's rifle cracked again, and one of the flankers on his side of the herd was thrown forward in his saddle when the slug loosed by Ki caught him high in the shoulder. The man did not fall to the ground, but slumped down on the shoulders of his mount.

Jessie was swinging the Winchester's muzzle to cover the second drag-rider when another rifle shot broke the air. The slug whistled past her, only inches from her head. Ki fired again but missed.

A rider dashed into sight from the front of the herd, a rifle in his hand. He saw Jessie and fired the rifle pistol-style, without shouldering it. His bullet missed Jessie, but whistled past her head so close that the wind of its passage fanned her ear. Before she could swing the Winchester's muzzle to aim at him, the man who'd fired the shot wheeled his mount around and spurred back into the herd.

Spooked by the shooting, the steers were beginning to mill now. The rustlers who'd been riding as flankers were spurring their horses into the center of the herd, seeking cover. Most of them were trying to make themselves less visible by bending forward in their saddles, lying on the shoulders of their mounts.

Jessie did not waste time trying to pick them off. She'd learned that an enemy stretched out on the neck of a horse is unable to shoulder a rifle, or use a pistol effectively. She glanced beyond the milling cattle, looking for Ki. He was nowhere in sight, but his riderless horse was ambling parallel to the herd. Knowing Ki's fighting tactics, Jessie realized that he'd dismounted voluntarily, to use the *ninja* tactics of which he was a master.

She looked for another target, but the men who'd been riding as flankers on her side of the herd were following the example set by their companions. They were stretching out on their horses' necks and spurring into the confused mass of milling steers where they would make difficult targets for even such an expert shot as Jessie.

"Dejen los ganados!" she heard one of the rustlers call. *"Desparnárrense! Escóndense al lado y maten los gringos!"*

Hearing the command for the rustlers to ride away from the milling cattle and take cover was enough warning for Jessie. She knew that Ki would also hear the rustler's shout, and was sure that he'd follow the tactics they'd used before when they'd been caught in an exposed position and outnumbered by enemies.

She dug her heels into Sun's flanks, and the big palomino began moving through the confused mass of milling cattle. Jessie prodded Sun's flank with her heel, and the horse turned obediently in the direction of Ki's riderless horse, which had stopped beside the trail.

By this time the shouts and shots had started the cattle to scattering. The steers were no longer a compact herd. Alarmed by the noise, they were beginning to string out. The rustlers were still scattering in obedience to the command of their leader, spurring for the cover of the broken country that bordered the trail.

Leaving Sun to pick his way through the milling steers, Jessie looked for Ki. She saw him at last. He was lying motionless, face down on the ground, a dozen yards away at the edge of the trail.

Chapter 3

Keeping her eyes on Ki, Jessie guided Sun with the pressure of her knees through the milling steers until she reached the spot where he was lying motionless. She glanced around quickly at the rustlers. They were scattered, obeying the command given them by their leader to seek the protection of the buttes.

She reached Ki's prone form, twitched the reins to halt the palomino, and swung out of her saddle to kneel beside Ki. A quick glance told her there was no blood staining the back of his jacket or trousers and no bullet wound in his back, and she tugged at his shoulders, turning him to lie on his back. No blood showed on the front of his clothing, but Ki's eyes were closed and there was a large red welt on his forehead.

Jessie grabbed her canteen and poured water into her palm and splashed it into Ki's face. He stirred, but did not open his eyes. A rifle cracked from one of the buttes, and the bullet plowed into the dirt inches away from where Jessie was kneeling. She knew that she had no time to waste. A glance around showed her that most of the rustlers had found cover, and the few who were still riding would be in protected positions within moments.

Bending down, Jessie got her hands into Ki's armpits and started to lift him, intending to hoist him on Sun's back and ride to safety. She was lifting him when Ki stirred and she felt the muscles of his back and arms ripple into life. Then his eyes opened and he looked up at her.

"I'm all right, Jessie," he said. He glanced around as he muscled himself to his feet with a movement that showed he'd regained his normal agility. "I was trying to crawl through the herd and get closer to the rustlers when a steer kicked me in the head." As he spoke, Ki glanced around at the clear area between them and the buttes and went on: "We'd better find some cover, too. Get back on Sun and I'll ride behind you."

Even before Jessie finished speaking two quick shots in succession cracked from the rifle of a rustler who'd found a protected position. Both of the bullets whistled above the heads of Jessie and Ki, but one grazed the cantle of Sun's saddle and left a tiny bright trough in the well-tanned leather before whistling off into the hard earth beyond the palomino. Jessie wasted no time in mounting, and Ki was astride Sun's rump almost as soon as she'd settled into the saddle.

"Go, Sun!" Jessie called, and the big palomino responded with a jumping start that took them across the clearing and into the broken country that bordered it.

Two or three shots sounded from the rifles of the rustlers as Sun carried Jessie and Ki into the maze of small buttes through which the trail wound. Jessie saw a mound high enough and long enough to shelter both them and the palomino, and toed Sun's flank to turn him behind it. Then she reined in.

"That was a little bit close," Ki remarked as he swung off Sun's back and bounced numbly to the ground.

Jessie was dismounting, too. She replied, "More than a

little bit, Ki. Too close for comfort. I wish we'd had time to get your horse, but I didn't see him. We could use the rifle in your saddle scabbard when these rustlers come after us."

"I'll try to whistle him up," Ki said. He puckered his lips and let out an eerie low-pitched, two-toned whistle. After a moment or so he repeated it. Then he told Jessie, "Unless he's wounded or dead, my horse will be here pretty quickly. You didn't happen to've seen him, I suppose?"

"I got a glimpse of him once," Jessie said. "That was just after the rustlers started shooting."

"He'll be around somewhere," Ki nodded. He repeated the same jagged-edged low-pitched whistle he'd sounded before. "I've trained him to come to that *komuso* whistle."

"We'll need your rifle if the rustlers attack us," Jessie went on. "They're certainly not going to just fade away."

"No. If they wanted the steers enough to steal them, I'm sure they'll fight to keep them," Ki agreed.

"I think I got two of them," Jessie went on. "But that still leaves six for us to deal with."

"We've been up against worse odds. And if we'd had our own choice you couldn't've picked a better place than these buttes."

"I didn't exactly choose it," Jessie reminded him. "It was the only place close enough to run for."

While they talked, Jessie and Ki had been inspecting their surroundings. Although its selection by Jessie had been a matter of expediency—the little butte being the nearest one which would shield the two of them and Sun —it was one which they might equally well have chosen if time had allowed them a wider choice.

At its base the butte was twenty or thirty feet thick, and Jessie remembered having noted that the side facing the rustler gang had been undercut at the base, making the front side virtually impossible to scale. The crest of the little formation towered above their heads, and while the wall on the side where they now stood was almost as vertical as the front, there was a slanting rise at the base which would give them footing while they shot over its top.

On the end nearest the area where the rustlers had taken cover, the edge of the butte zigzagged like stairs from bottom to top, and Jessie saw at once that the shape of the formation provided a protected position that would enable her and Ki both to shoot at the same time. At the opposite end the butte curved into a hook like the letter J laid on its side. Within the curved area there was room for the two of them to take cover if the rustlers tried to attack from both sides at once.

"We can hold them off here as long as our ammunition lasts," Jessie said as they finished examining their sheltered position.

"And from the way they're moving around out there, I'd guess that's what we're going to be doing in a very few minutes," Ki told her. He'd moved down to the jagged end of the butte to watch their enemies. "It looks very much like they're getting ready to come after us."

Jessie joined Ki and looked toward the broken area to which the rustlers had retreated after the first exchange of shots. If they were planning an attack, there was no sign that they were assembling. Through the sparse growth of lechuguilla and creosote brush, neither of them growing close together or more than shoulder-high, they could get an occasional glimpse of a moving figure. None of the moving men exposed himself for more than a split second, and Jessie was too combat-wise to waste her scarce supply of rifle ammunition by shooting at such uncertain targets.

"They're professionals, all right," Ki commented. "My

guess is that they're veterans of some of the Mexican revolutions, turned outlaw."

"Yes. They act like they've had a lot of experience at this kind of thing," Jessie agreed. She studied the terrain from which the shots had come, then went on: "That area where we see them moving is three or four hundred feet away, Ki. I'm not going to risk wasting ammunition on chance shots, if that's what they're trying to tempt us to do."

"I don't think that's their idea, Jessie. You only fired three shots, but they learned a lesson from them. I'm sure they're planning to attack us, but when they do it's not going to be all of them rushing us in a bunch."

"If they do rush us, I've got plenty of shells," Jessie assured him. "Both for the rifle and my Colt. They're in my saddlebags."

"I've got six *shuriken* in my sleeve case," Ki said, "and more in my saddlebags. There's still a chance my horse will show up, so I might have a rifle, too. But even without it, we ought to be able to account for what's left of the rustler gang."

"Speaking of saddlebags, I'd better get mine before those rustlers begin to close in on us," Jessie went on. "And I wish there was a sheltered place where I could put Sun. If those outlaws should shoot him—"

"They're more likely to want to keep him for themselves when they see him," Ki said. "And we'd better keep him close to us. If things get really tight, we might need him for a getaway."

Jessie stepped over to the palomino and reached for the saddlebag in which she carried her ammunition. She had her hand on the capacious leather pouch where she carried her spare ammunition before she noticed how shrunken and limp it was. Then she saw the ripped and shredded gap in

29

the leather of its bottom where a near-miss bullet had struck the bag and torn through it, letting its contents spill out. Although she knew it was a useless gesture, Jessie lifted the bag and hefted it, feeling its flabby emptiness. Then she turned and stepped back to the butte.

"We've been a little too optimistic," she told Ki. "One of those rustlers' stray shots went through my saddlebag. The one on the side where I carry my spare ammunition is empty. We'll have to get along with the shells that're left in my rifle and pistol."

Ki's expression did not change when Jessie broke the bad news to him. He nodded and said, "I suppose we'll make do, one way or another. How many shells do you have left?"

"Three in the rifle and five in my Colt."

"And I have my six *shuriken*. That should be enough, if we're careful not to let them fool us into wasting shots."

"It'll have to be enough, Ki. If these men are like most of the Mexican outlaw gangs we've run into, they're not going to press us too hard at first."

Ki nodded. "You're right. They'll snipe at us for a while, then try to keep us off-balance with some feints, tempting us to waste ammunition. And if those tactics don't work, they'll rush us as a last resort."

A shot sounded from the mesa's downslope. The flank of the huge, flat-topped rise had little more vegetation than the ground at its base, but it supported small clumps of thick-growing scrub cedar and patches of waist-high prickly pear. Jessie and Ki knew when the outlaws had reached cover, because the rustlers began firing when they hid on the mesa's sloping flank.

Rifles cracked from the concealing growth, and bullets thunked into the wall of the butte high over Jessie's head. The first outburst of shots was followed by a second ragged fusillade from a spot thirty or forty yards distant from the covering brush cedar where the first had originated.

Jessie said, "I counted eleven shots, Ki."

"So did I." Ki pointed to the downslope that stretched away from them toward the base of the mesa a bit more than a quarter of a mile distant, where wispy, widely-separated fingers of gunsmoke were drifting lazily upward. "At least we know that there are two bunches of them, and we know where they're holed up."

Before Jessie could reply, another ragged volley of riflefire sounded from the mesa's side. More hot lead plowed into the high dirt wall above their heads.

Her voice as cool as though she was commenting on some trivial matter of little importance, Jessie said, "And that accounts for the second bunch."

"About half those rifles they're using are old French army Chassepots." Ki frowned. "I got a good look at them while we were closing in on them. Besides, there's no other gun in the world that has that flat report when it's fired."

Jessie did not question Ki's identification of the weapons the rustlers were using. She knew from past experience that he'd studied weaponry extensively.

"They've got a long range, though," she commented.

"Yes," Ki nodded. "They're long-range, but single-shots, and slow to reload. Those rustlers aren't fools or scared, Jessie. They just know the limitations of the guns they've got."

"And they don't know we're short of ammunition," Jessie nodded. "That gives us another tiny edge, Ki."

"Which we need," Ki agreed. "My guess is that they'll test us out and keep us pinned down here, hoping we'll waste our ammunition returning their fire. Then when they think the time's right, they'll rush us."

Another ragged volley came from the slope where the rustlers were concealed. More dirt trickled down from the wall of the butte, but only one or two of the rifle-slugs came close to them.

"They might be planning to keep us pinned down here until dark." Jessie frowned. "And then we could be in real trouble instead of just a bit uncomfortable."

Ki nodded. "That's occurred to me. But if they do pin us down here all day, we've got plenty of time to figure out how to get away fast when the light starts to fail."

"I don't like to think about retreating, Ki," Jessie protested. "We didn't follow that gang to—" She broke off and pointed toward the slope where the outlaws had holed up. "It looks to me like they might be getting reinforcements."

Ki turned to follow Jessie's pointing finger. On the rim of the mesa, above the long slope of its walls where the rustlers had taken up their stations, a horseman had suddenly appeared. In the distance that lay between him and the butte where Jessie and Ki had taken refuge, he was just a dark figure silhouetted against the bright morning sky. All that they could tell about him was that he wore a broad-brimmed hat and a long, cloaklike coat or duster that fell in folds almost to his stirrups.

"There doesn't seem to be anybody with him," Ki said. "But you might be right, Jessie. Maybe he's the man who—"

Ki broke off as another ragged volley of shots came from the rustlers on the slope of the mesa. Again he and Jessie ducked behind the butte as bullets whistled over their heads or thunked into the outcropping ledge where they were standing.

Remembering how a second volley had followed the first when the rustlers had fired before, Jessie and Ki kept their heads low. The fresh volley came quicker this time. The rolling crack of the rustlers' rifles sounded again, and still more rifle-slugs plowed into the baked earth above them.

"They only fired twice the last time," Ki said. He raised his head and gazed at the mesa. "And I don't—" He stopped suddenly and then exclaimed, "Jessie! Look!"

Jessie had been slower than Ki in raising her head after the second round of shots from the outlaws. She lifted it now and followed Ki's pointing finger.

At the rim of the mesa the strange rider had dismounted and was shedding his long duster. He tossed it across his saddle and started down the sloping side. As he moved, he was drawing pistols from the holsters that were now visible low on each hip. He moved with long strides, jumping rather than running, as he angled across the slanting face of the wide mesa.

"What on earth—" Jessie began. Then she broke off as the stranger brought up his revolvers and began firing as he advanced with long leaping strides down the steep slope.

"That's where one bunch of those rustlers was holed up!" Ki exclaimed. "I don't know who that man is, Jessie, but he's certainly not one of the rustlers!"

Distant shouts now broke the air, punctuating the evenly spaced shots from the stranger's revolvers, as the man continued his advance. He did not slow down, but when the rustlers began to return his fire he started zigzagging instead of moving in a straight line as he had in the beginning.

Puffs of powdersmoke began spurting from the mesa's face, and tiny dust-clouds rose from the ground on both sides of the lone shootist as the rustlers began to return his fire. The stranger did not interrupt his zigzag advance.

"He's shooting the rustlers!" Jessie exclaimed as she

33

saw the little group of cattle-thieves who'd boiled out of their hiding place fall one by one as the newcomer's lead went home.

"And he's a dead shot, too," Ki said, his eyes still fixed on the scene that was unfolding on the steep flank of the mesa.

"But who is he and where did he come from?" Jessie asked, without turning away from the mesa.

"I suppose we'll find out pretty soon, if he manages to stay alive," Ki told her. "All I'm sure of right now is that he showed up at the right time and saw we were in trouble."

They fell silent, their eyes fixed on the mesa. The stranger was changing his course now, heading toward the second group of rustlers, who'd entrenched themselves on the slope. They'd taken up a position fifty yards from the members of the band who'd already fallen to the newcomer's deadly revolvers.

"We've got to help him, Ki!" Jessie exclaimed. She grabbed her rifle and swung it to cover the second bunch of rustlers. One of them was raising a revolver, aiming it at the advancing man.

Jessie got the outlaw in her sights and squeezed off a shot before the rustler could trigger his revolver. The cattle-thief's body jerked as the Winchester's bullet caught him. Then he fell backward. The outlaw's dying reflex cramped his hand as he toppled from the impact of Jessie's slug, and the shot he'd intended to bring down the stranger went off, the bullet going up into empty air.

By now the lone shootist was within range of the remaining rustlers. He started firing again, shooting unhurriedly as they began to swing their long, clumsy Chassepot rifles toward him. The shots from the man advancing toward them took the cattle-thieves one at a time before any

34

of them could discard the rifles and draw their holstered revolvers.

"This is one of the most amazing things I've ever seen!" Jessie exclaimed as the echoes of gunfire died away. "Who could that man be, Ki?"

"I'm sure I don't know either," Ki answered. "But he got here just at the right time. Luckily for us, he had a notion to help us."

"But how could he know—" Jessie started. Then she broke off. Her eyes were still fixed on the flank of the mesa, and she saw the stranger turning back from the brush where the rustlers had been hidden, and climbing the mesa's wall toward his horse. "It looks like he's leaving, Ki! We've got to catch up with him and find out who he is and why he stopped to help us!"

Ki nodded. "Yes, of course we do, Jessie. Mount up, and I'll ride postillion again. We can look for my horse later; he can't be very far from here."

Sun's sturdy legs quickly carried them up the mesa's sloping side. As they neared its top ridgeline they saw the stranger standing beside his own horse, calmly taking cartridges from his saddlebags and reloading one of his pistols. He looked up when he saw Jessie and Ki approaching, nodded, and went on with his job of reloading.

By the time they were within speaking distance he'd finished filling the cylinder of one of his weapons, and he replaced it in his holster. He was reloading the second revolver when Jessie reined Sun to a halt. She and Ki had been studying the stranger as they approached. He was a tall man, broad-shouldered, with lean, sunken cheeks that bore a traveler's stubble, and a full mustache, which hid his mouth. Under the broad brim of his hat a pair of cold blue eyes looked at them.

Jessie spoke first. "My name's Jessica Starbuck. Those

outlaws you shot had rustled a herd of cattle from my Circle Star ranch and were heading for the border with them."

"Yes, ma'am," the stranger replied. He closed the loading port of his Remington Frontier revolver and replaced it in its holster. "I saw a few head of your steers on the flat down below and figured out from the brand what was happening."

"Well, I don't know how to thank you for what you did to help me," Jessie went on. "But I'll be glad to pay you a substantial reward."

"That's very thoughtful of you, Miss Starbuck," the man replied. "But I don't expect a reward in cash money."

Jessie frowned and said, "I'm afraid I don't understand."

"Maybe you will when I explain," the man told her. "You see, I was on my way to your ranch when I heard you and the rustlers shooting. I've been doing a lot of thinking while I was over in Mexico, and it looks to me like you're the best person in the country that I can go to for some help I need myself."

"I'm getting even more confused," Jessie admitted. "I'm sure we haven't met before. Or have we?"

"No, ma'am, Miss Starbuck. We sure haven't," the stranger replied. "But you've likely heard about me. Permit me to introduce myself. My name is Frank James."

Chapter 4

Jessie's jaw dropped in sudden surprise, and even the usually stoical Ki opened his eyes wider when he heard the name by which the stranger had introduced himself.

"You—you mean Frank James, the outlaw?" Jessie gasped.

The man nodded. "Well, some folks call me an outlaw."

"And you're telling us you're Jesse James's brother?" Jessie asked after a long pause.

"That's right, Miss Starbuck. But he's back in Missouri —or was the last I heard. I got a letter just before I started up from Mexico for the border."

"And you were coming to the Circle Star? To see me?" Jessie asked, trying to conceal the amazement that was creeping into her voice. "What on earth for?"

"Well, now, if you'll indulge me a mite, I'd like to wait for a better time to tell you all about that," the man who'd called himself Frank James replied. "But first off, let me say just one thing. I've led a real mean life, and nobody knows it any better than I do. What I'll ask you to believe is that for the past six months or so, since I've been in Mexico, I've made a firm vow to give up all the lawless

37

ways Jesse and I have been following for such a long time."

"I'd be the last to hold any doubts as to your good intentions, Mr. James," Jessie said. "But what about your brother? Is he going to join you?"

"We'll be leaving together," Frank James answered. "Just like we joined up with Quantrill together when the war broke out. We've been together all our lives and we aim to stay together."

"I'd like to believe you, Mr.—Mr. James," Jessie said when the outlaw paused. "But I'm afraid it's going to take a lot to convince me that you're who you say you are, and that if you really are Frank James you're going to quit your outlaw life."

"I don't have a single right to expect you'd believe me, Miss Starbuck," the stranger said. "And that's been bothering me quite a lot since I made up my mind to talk to you."

Jessie had seldom felt at such a loss for words. For almost her entire life she'd heard of the James brothers, and their long and lurid careers as bank robbers, train robbers, killers, and outlaws. Now when she met a man who claimed quite casually to be one of the two notorious brothers, she could think of nothing to ask him that would confirm his claim or discredit it.

"Oh, I'll give you chapter and verse when the time comes," the stranger assured her.

Jessie's years of following in her father's footsteps, in business and finance as well as in facing and defeating the enemies who'd murdered him, had given her a good grasp of human nature. She'd come to feel that she could determine truth from falsehood with quick intuition and reasonable accuracy. But this time she wasn't sure.

When she remained silent, the stranger picked up the thread of their conversation. He said, "I'd imagine you're a lot more concerned right now about bunching your cattle than you are about hearing me talk. I've done a little bit of cowhanding in my day, and I'll be glad to help you and your man."

"Of course I want to gather my steers, but I—" Jessie stopped short, suddenly at a total loss for words. When neither Ki nor the man who'd called himself Frank James made an effort to pick up the conversation, she reached a quick decision and went on. "Very well, Mr. James. At least for the moment I'll believe you're who you say you are, and I'll certainly accept your offer to help us. And I'm sorry that I neglected to introduce you to Ki."

"Oh, I know who Ki is." The stranger nodded. "You just might be surprised at how many times both of your names are mentioned in the kind of company I've kept most of my life."

This time Jessie managed to keep from showing her amazement. Now Ki bridged what might have been an awkward moment between Jessie and the man. He said, "We'd certainly appreciate your help, Mr. James. We could bunch up the stolen steers by ourselves, but three of us can do it lots faster."

"From what I've heard about you, Ki, you're sort of Miss Starbuck's strawboss," the man said. "Go on and tell me what you want me to do, and I'll buckle down just like I was one of your regular hands."

"We'd better start by circling," Ki replied. "If you'll slant down the side of the mesa toward the southeast, Jessie and I will go the other way and start chousing the steers into a bunch down below on level ground."

"It won't be any job at all, Ki." James, or his namesake, nodded. "There's not enough high brush here on the slope or down below to hide any of 'em. With all three of us working, we can clean up this mess in no time at all."

"By the way," Ki went on, "if you run across a dark bay pony with a Circle Star brand on it, whistle or call. He'll be mine."

Jessie had been listening to the businesslike conversation between Ki and the stranger with growing amazement. She was still very much surprised that any man in his right mind would claim to be a notorious outlaw, and the stranger's remark about being headed for the Circle Star had started her wondering if she was the intended victim of some sort of confidence game.

For as long as Jessie could remember, she'd heard and read about the James brothers. Their criminal activities had been the subject of stories in almost every newspaper, and the James Boys and their gang had been a topic of discussion in virtually all the many places that she'd visited during the traveling she'd had to do in supervising the far-flung Starbuck empire built by her father.

To have encountered someone claiming to be Frank James in such an unlikely place, to have seen him display the legendary marksmanship with a pistol that was commonly attributed to the outlaw, and then to have him remark almost casually that he'd been planning to visit her, added to the shock from which she was just recovering.

Jessie's surprise had not been lessened by the stranger's manner of speech. Instead of the gruffness and heedless grammar of so many men she'd encountered on the Western frontier, his style of speaking was both literate and reasonably grammatical, which marked him as a well educated man by the standards of the place and time.

It was not Jessie's way to delay a decision. She decided, for the moment at least, to accept the newcomer as the man he claimed to be. She said, "We've got the bodies of those outlaws to bury, too, Mr. James. Should we do that first, before we start trying to round up my cattle?"

"Why, I don't imagine it'd make much difference, Miss Starbuck," James replied. "But if it was left up to me, I'd get after the steers first. They'll be scattered all over hell's half-acre—excuse me, ma'am." The outlaw's face reddened for a moment, and he bowed his head in embarrassment. Then he went on: "Like I was saying when my tongue slipped, your steers are going to scatter out right bad if we don't get after them."

Jessie nodded. "We'll leave the burying until later, then. Maybe Ki and I better do that while you keep the herd shaped up after we've finished the gathers."

"Suppose I ride downslope with you, Jessie," Ki said. "If we have any luck, we'll find my horse pretty quickly, and even if we don't, I can ride one of the outlaws' horses. Then I can help Mr. James with the gathers while you shape up the herd and keep the steers from scattering again."

"That sounds fine," Jessie said. Her equanimity was returning fast. "And I suppose the quicker we get to work, the quicker we'll get started back to the Circle Star."

Frank James replied with a nod, stepped over to his horse, and swung into the saddle. He touched the broad brim of his hat to Jessie, dug his heels into the animal's flanks, and started down the sloping mesa face without wasting time.

"Do you think he could really be Frank James?" Jessie asked Ki as they watched him ride off.

"I've been asking myself that ever since he mentioned his name," Ki replied. "And I'm as uncertain as you seem to be, Jessie. What do you plan to do?"

"I haven't any plan at all yet," she said. "He's not the kind of man I'd expect Frank James to be, but there's something about him that's got me halfway to believing that he's telling us the truth."

41

Ki frowned. "There must be some way we can find out."

"I don't know what it'd be," Jessie told him. "But even if he is some kind of confidence man trying to use me for one of his schemes, I'm going along with him for a while. Now, if we're going to get those steers bunched, we'd better get moving, too."

Jessie swung into Sun's saddle, and Ki vaulted up onto the palomino's rump. She reined the big stallion down the mesa's slope. Looking toward the man about whom she and Ki had just been talking, she said over her shoulder, "Whoever or whatever he is—Frank James the outlaw or some kind of confidence man—he knows how to handle a horse."

"What do you think, Jessie? Is he or isn't he?" Ki asked.

"I don't know, Ki. What he's told us has the ring of truth, but I can't imagine why an outlaw like Frank James would be coming to visit me at the Circle Star."

"He didn't offer much confirmation, at that," Ki agreed. "But he didn't hesitate once while we were talking."

"Well, I'll turn your question back to you," Jessie said. "Do you think he's told us the truth?"

"I'm as undecided as you are," Ki replied. "In one way, I'm inclined to believe him. In another way, I feel as you do, and wonder what on earth a man like Frank James would be coming to talk to you about."

"Whatever his proposition is will be the acid test," Jessie said. "I've been the target of so many confidence men —just as Alex was—that I think I can smell one a mile off."

"And this fellow didn't have the smell?" Ki asked.

"That's one of the things I'm not sure about yet," Jessie

said. "But I'm willing to listen for a while to whatever he has to say. That's when I'll be sure."

They rode on in silence through the afternoon stillness. As they drew closer to the bottom of the mesa's sloping side, the blatting of steers grew louder and they saw the backs of Circle Star cattle above the thin, low brush. They'd almost reached level ground when Ki touched Jessie's shoulder and pointed.

"There's my horse, Jessie! Right over next to that little bunch of steers. Rein over, and I'll get busy. And if our new volunteer can work cattle as he claims he can, we'll have the herd bunched up before it's too dark to see."

"I hope you're right, Ki. Because if we can gather all those loose steers before it gets too dark, we'll be back on the trail to the ranch as soon as it's light enough to see."

"There we are, Ki," the man who called himself Frank James said. He gave a final twist to the last strand of barbwire they'd been splicing in the Circle Star boundary fence to close the gap cut by the rustler gang. Then he turned to Jessie and went on: "It's not very pretty splice, but it's the best I can do without any tools and working in the dark this way."

"I'll have one of the hands come out early tomorrow and string new wire," Ki said. "But we're home again, and I can't say I'm sorry."

Jessie had been standing in the center of the gap to keep any of the steers from straying away while the barbwire was being spliced. The three had found little time to talk since they'd begun rounding up the Circle Star cattle. After chousing the steers into a compact herd, Jessie had kept them bunched while Ki and James hastily buried the bodies of the dead rustlers.

Then they'd divided to do night-herd duty, two circling

the herd on horseback for two hours at a watch while the third slept. Night-herding had kept them separated, and precluded any conversation between the two who stayed awake, for the cattle were still nervous and needed to be watched constantly.

With the first faint tinge of dawn they'd started the steers moving toward the Circle Star range. Jessie rode point, leading the way. Frank James volunteered to ride drag and refused to listen to Ki's suggestion that the two men split up the hours of riding at the back of the herd and swallowing its dust. Ki had inherited the flanker's position by default, and had spent the long day circling the steers and keeping them in a more or less compact formation.

Now, with the night two hours old, the cattle safely back on the ranch's southeast range, and the fence cut by the rustlers mended, all three were feeling a letdown after the hard days they'd just spent.

"Let's go on to the house, Ki," Jessie said. "Mr. James is going to stay with us while he explains the reason he came looking for me."

Ki nodded. He and Jessie had worked together for such a long time that neither of them needed a long-winded explanation to understand the hidden meaning of such a seemingly innocuous statement as the one Jessie had just made. In the inflection of Jessie's voice, he'd gotten the real meaning behind her words:

"I'll trust this man who calls himself Frank James until I hear what he has to say," she was telling him. *"But we'll both watch him closely until we're satisfied that he's telling the truth instead of lying."*

"I appreciate your hospitality, Miss Starbuck," James said. "And I'm sure that after you've heard what I have to say you'll understand why I've decided to come to you."

"I'm looking forward to hearing your story, Mr. James,"

Jessie told him. "I'm sure it'll be interesting. But right now all I can think about is washing off the trail-dust and getting some sleep. I'm sure you feel the same way."

"Well, when Jesse and I rode with the gang, I learned how to go for a long time without closing my eyes," James replied. "Which doesn't mean that I won't be grateful for a bed."

They mounted up then, and started for the Circle Star main house, still almost three hours' ride away. They talked very little as they pushed through the starlit darkness. Ki rode ahead to handle the two or three gates that remained to be opened and closed, and by the time they'd gotten to the main house and the headquarters buildings that clustered around it the night was well along.

Some of the light sleepers in the bunkhouse had been roused by the hoofbeats of the trio's horses and were waiting in the open space between the bunkhouse, cookhouse, and main house when the three weary riders reined in. Two of the men carried lanterns. Rance Sanders, the foreman, was one of them. He stepped up to Jessie's horse as she dismounted.

"Manny told us about the rustlers," Sanders said. "I hope you and Ki caught up with them."

"We did. And we got the herd they'd taken and drove it back," she replied. "It's safe on the southwest range again."

"I bet you folks are sure tired, Miss Jessie," Sanders went on. "Now, you let me and the boys look after your horses. You and Ki and your friend can go right on in the house and settle down."

"Thank you, Rance," Jessie replied. "I'll tell you the whole story tomorrow."

While Jessie and the foreman were talking, Ki and Frank James had dismounted. One of the hands carrying a lantern stepped up to hold the light while they took their saddlebags off the rumps of their horses. He followed them when they stepped aside to wait for Jessie to finish her brief conversation with Sanders. As James and Ki turned to follow Jessie to the main house, he put a hand on Ki's arm.

"Would you wait just a minute, Ki?" he asked. "There's something I need to talk to you about."

"Can we wait until tomorrow, Cord?" Ki asked.

"It'd be a lot better if we talked tonight."

"All right." Ki called to Jessie, "You go ahead, Jessie, and get our guest settled in. I'll be along in a minute." He turned back to Cord and said, "Now, then. What's on your mind?"

Cord frowned. "That fellow that rode in with you—Did he tell you who he is?"

"He gave us a name," Ki replied. "Why?"

"I bet it wasn't his real one, then," the ranch hand went on. "Because I know who he is. Ki, that fellow's Frank James, the outlaw! Jesse James' brother!"

"Are you sure?" Ki asked.

"Damn right, I'm sure!" Cord retorted. "I've seen him and Jesse more'n once. Before I headed down here to Texas, I handed for Nigger John's horse farm up in Wyoming Territory. That's where Frank and Jesse James' gang got their horses, Ki."

"Maybe you'd better tell me a little bit more about how you got acquainted with the Jameses," Ki suggested.

"Why, there ain't much to tell." Cord frowned. "I got turned outta my job in Rock Springs, where I'd been a deputy sheriff. A new sheriff got elected, so when Nigger John asked me if I'd like to go to work for him, I told him I sure would."

"Wait a minute," Ki broke in. "This Nigger John, was he really a black man?"

"Oh, sure. That's why everybody called him Nigger John; his name was John Trammell. He was an emancipated slave, and if there was ever a man that knew about horses, it was him. But after I'd worked for him a little while, these two men come riding in late one night, and their horses was blowed and they had five or six more on lead ropes. Nigger John rousted me and his other helper outta bed, and we cut out a string of fresh horses in the dark, and them fellows rode off with 'em right away."

"That's when you learned the two men were Frank and Jesse James?" Ki asked.

Cord nodded. "It sure was. Because about a week later I heard about how the James gang had robbed the westbound Limited up by Medicine Bow."

"But this John Trammell, he never did tell you that the men who got the horses were the James brothers?" Ki frowned.

Cord shook his head. "Nary a word from Nigger John about who them two fellows were. But the other wrangler that worked on the horse farm told me they was Frank and Jesse James."

"You only saw the James brothers once, then?" Ki asked.

"Hell, no! They come back three or four times afterwards, and every time it was like the first one. They'd ride in on horses that had been run hard, and got fresh ones. Oh, I know Frank James when I see him, you can bet on that! And he's the man that rode in with you and he's in the main house right now with Miss Jessie!"

Chapter 5

Ki stood silently for a moment, debating the course he should follow. Then he said, "The man who rode in with Jessie and me told us right away that he's Frank James."

"I knew I was right!" Cord burst out. "Even if it's been a while since I seen him and Jesse. They ain't the kind a fellow forgets about."

"Now, I'm not going to ask you to keep quiet about this," Ki went on. "It'd be too much to expect, and from what James told us, he won't kick up any fuss about you men in the bunkhouse knowing who he is."

"Ki, do you mind telling me how you and Jessie happened to run into him?" Cord asked.

"I don't suppose Jessie would object," Ki replied slowly. "We'd caught up with the rustlers and were in the middle of a fight with them when he came along and gave us a hand."

"Is he as good with a gun as he's supposed to be?" Cord asked, his eyes wide open with excitement.

"Better," Ki told him. "But I know that Jessie wouldn't want you men treating James differently from any of the other guests who've been here. Just speak to him if you run into him, and go on about your business. And you'd better warn the men to keep your talk about him inside the bunk-house."

"Sure." Cord nodded. "I can see why Miss Jessie'd want to keep his being here sorta private."

"I'll be getting to bed, then," Ki said. "Thanks for telling me what you knew, Cord. It might come in handy."

A lamp had been lighted in the entrance hall of the rambling stone main house, which Alex Starbuck had built before his brutal murder at the hands of cartel assassins. Beyond the hallway, Ki saw light spilling from the study, which was Jessie's favorite room. He covered the few steps required to reach the doorway and looked inside. Jessie was curled up in the big leather upholstered chair which her father had favored. Her head rested on the back of the chair and her eyes were closed.

"Jessie?" Ki said, keeping his voice low.

Jessie opened her eyes and looked at him. "What delayed you outside, Ki? I hope it wasn't more trouble."

"No. I've been talking to one of the hands—Cord, the one who hired on about eight months ago, from Wyoming Territory. He says that our guest really is Frank James."

"How on earth could he be sure?" Jessie was sitting erect now, her eyes wide open, all her sleepiness gone.

"Cord said he used to work on a horse farm in Wyoming," Ki explained. "One where Frank and Jesse James got horses for their gang. He told me he'd seen both of them a number of times."

"You believed him?"

Ki nodded. "Yes, I did, Jessie. It's not the kind of story that a ranch hand like Cord would have the imagination to make up. He said he recognized Frank James immediately, and after you two had left he took me off to one side to warn me who it was that we'd brought here with us. Then he went on to explain exactly how he was able to recognize

49

James, and his whole story hung together. I'm sure he told the truth."

Jessie nodded, then said, "You know, Ki, I didn't have any doubt that we were looking at the real Frank James after seeing the way he wiped out those rustlers singlehandedly. I have never seen a man shoot like that before."

"Yes, his shooting went a long way to convince me, too," Ki agreed.

"Well, I'm going to bed now," Jessie said as she got up and stretched. "And tomorrow we'll find out why James was coming here and what he has in mind. Outlaw or not, after the help he gave us with those rustlers, we owe him a lot more than just listening to him."

"I think it's time for me to listen to your story now, Mr. James," Jessie told her guest as she pushed aside her breakfast plate the following morning.

While at the breakfast table, she'd had her first chance to study Frank James more closely that had been possible before. During the time spent driving the recovered steers back to the Circle Star range, the three had been apart almost every minute of the daylight hours.

Jessie saw now that the outlaw was older than he'd appeared to be during their brief contacts while they'd bunched the steers and started them home. He still wore the rumpled coat and smudged white collarless shirt that he'd had on the previous day, but he'd added a vest to his brown coat, and this morning the bulge of only one revolver-butt showed under the coat. He was taller than he'd seemed to be on horseback, and now that his broad-brimmed hat no longer shaded his face, his nose showed the hump of an old break above his thick nostrils.

James' dark brown hair was beginning to thin out, and there were white hairs visible at his temples as well as in the full mustache that extended in sharp points beyond the corners of his thin lips. She noticed also that he had a network of fine lines at the outer corners of his eyes, which seemed more prominent now that they were indoors and he no longer had to squint under bright sunshine as he had the previous day. The lines at his eyes showed now like fine white crisscrossed threads against his tanned skin.

"I think we'll find the study more comfortable than these straight chairs in here," Jessie went on as she stood up. "And I'm sure you won't object if Ki joins us."

"After seeing the way you two were working together holding off that bunch of rustlers, I halfway expected you'd want him to be around," James said. "It reminded me a great deal of the way Jesse and I have worked together so many times. Or do you find my comparison objectionable, Miss Starbuck?"

"It doesn't offend me," Jessie replied. "But Ki will have to answer for himself."

"I don't have any objections," Ki said quickly. "And I'm as curious as Jessie is about your reason for wanting to talk to her. It must be something really important."

James nodded. "It is. It's important to me and Jesse both."

Alex's study—Jessie had never thought of it in any other terms; to her the room was still her father's—though spartan, was furnished luxuriously. One wall was dominated by bookshelves, all well filled; another by the massive fieldstone fireplace, dark now in the late days of summer. A large oil portrait of her mother hung above the mantel. Alex's portrait in oils, which hung on the wall opposite the fireplace, had been Jessie's only addition to the room. The room was furnished with deeply cushioned leather upholstered divan and easy chairs which Alex had chosen.

Jessie left Ki and Frank James to select their own seats. She went at once to the big burgundy-leather chair that had been Alex's favorite and settled into it. The chair had become her favorite, too, for it still held a faint ghostlike aroma of the cherry-flavored pipe tobacco that Alex had smoked.

Frank James chose to sit on the divan facing the chair that Jessie occupied. Ki sat at the opposite end of the divan. They looked at one another for a moment, then Jessie nodded at her guest.

"I'm ready to listen, Mr. James," she said.

"You know, I'm going to have to talk some about my brother, and there might be times when I'd confuse you a little bit because your name sounds the same as my brother's, even if it's spelled differently. Now, about half the time, when I talk to Jesse I call him by a nickname he had hung on him when he wasn't much more than a baby. It's Dingus. Suppose I just call him that when I'm talking about him."

"I certainly don't have any objections," Jessie replied. "And I'm sure Ki wouldn't, either."

"That's what I'll do, then." James nodded. He looked from Jessie to Ki for a moment, and after a grimace that was half smile, half frown, he said, "It's a little bit hard for me to get started on what I'm trying to say, Miss Starbuck. While I was riding up from our place in Mexico, I went over and over it in my mind, but I'll ask you to bear with me if I forget and have to go cut and try a little bit."

"Go ahead and tell your story in your own way, Mr. James," Jessie told the outlaw. "We're not in any hurry."

"People have told an awful lot of lies about Dingus and me," James began. "And there's been such a lot more that wasn't a bit true, printed in newspapers and dime novels, that I guess by now him and me are the only ones that

52

really know the facts about how we got to be outlaws. But I don't intend to lie to you, Miss Starbuck. I hope you'll take my bounden oath on that."

Jessie nodded. "You've convinced me that you're serious."

"Well, then," James went on, "I'd imagine you know that Dingus and I rode with Quantrill during the war. It wasn't some kind of Sunday-school picnic—not the way old Quantrill taught us how to fight. And since he didn't have any standing with the government—" He stopped and shook his head before adding, "Not that there was much government at all on the Confederate side, as far north as the country where Quantrill got started. And he was one mean man, Miss Starbuck, maybe the meanest one I have ever run into."

Frank James paused for breath and Jessie said, "I studied history, Mr. James. I know about Quantrill's Raiders."

"Sure." James nodded. "I guess everybody does now. But you won't find out the whole truth about Quantrill and us men that rode with him just by reading it in the books. There's plenty of things he did and that he made us do, but there's a lot more that's just not decent to print. All of that's gone by and back of us, anyways."

"It's not what you did during the war that we're talking about, Mr. James," Jessie said. "It's what you and your brothers have done since then."

James nodded and went on: "Well, when the war was over and Dingus and I got free of Quantrill's outfit, we had a go at farming. It was only sharecropping, though, and we were dead broke all the time. We just couldn't make it."

He paused, looking up at the *vigas* that spanned the room's ceiling, then continued: "There's not any use in giving you chapter and verse of the hard times we had, Miss Starbuck. When we rode with Quantrill, we lived off the land, and by that I don't mean robbing a farmer's fields of corn and potatoes and garden truck. We took whatever money we found in damn-yankee houses, and when we'd take a little town from the bluecoats we'd grab whatever money and jewelry we could find. Of course, that was all supposed to be handed over to Quantrill to trade for gunpowder and lead and rations, but some of it stuck to our hands."

James stopped again, obviously recalling the past. He sat silently for a moment. Ki said, "I think Jessie and I both understand your guerrilla days, Mr. James. As she just said, we've both studied history."

"Yes, I guess it's just history, now." James nodded. "I was just trying to explain how Dingus and I got started. And I'm sure you know what came next. After we'd put up with all the hard times we thought we could stand, we held up a little bank in a town up in Idaho—I forget the name of it now, it's been such a long time ago. And we got away without much trouble; you know we'd learned how to travel far and fast during our raider days. Anyways, we lived high for a while. Then it got a lot easier to hold up another bank, and a little while after that we ran into the Younger boys, Cole and Frank, when we went home to Missouri for a visit with what few kinfolks we had left. And that was how the James gang started."

When he paused, Jessie said, "Suppose we just accept the fact that you and your brother led a gang of outlaws who robbed banks and trains, Mr. James. You said that you had a good reason for coming to see me. I'd like to hear what it is."

"Well, to get right down to bedrock facts, Miss Starbuck, both Dingus and me are tired of outlaw life. Both of us are married men now, and Jesse's even got a family started. What we want to do is give up and hand back whatever's left of our loot to the authorities."

For several minutes both Jessie and Ki sat in silence after the outlaw had made his surprising statement. At last Jessie said, "I suppose both you and your brother have talked about this before you came looking for me?"

"Oh, sure. Except that Dingus doesn't know yet it was you that I'd hit on to talk to. Your name just popped into my mind while I was down in Mexico. That was after I'd been studying for a long time, trying to think of somebody that I could go to for help. And believe me, I thought of just about everybody from the president of the United States on down, Miss Starbuck. Then I was reading an old newspaper that somebody'd left at our ranch, and there was a piece in it about you."

Jessie smiled. "Yes, I suppose that Hetty Green and I are mentioned in the newspapers almost as often as actresses and opera singers."

"Well, I'd heard about you some before, but I didn't have any idea that Dingus and I would come to the giving-up point," James said. "Then after I'd read that newspaper piece, it came to me just all of a sudden that maybe you'd be the right one to talk to about my plan."

"Exactly what is your plan, Mr. James?" she asked.

"As much as I've thought about it, I'm not quite sure yet," he admitted. "I don't imagine you'd know about how it is with men like Dingus and me. We don't live in the same kind of world that law-abiding folks do. We've spent most of our lives outside the law, and it takes a lot of figuring to understand how it is with people who aren't always fighting or robbing or running."

Frank James fell silent again, and this time it was Ki who spoke:

"I think I can understand a bit about how you and your

55

brother feel, Mr. James. I was on the verge of becoming—well, not exactly an outlaw, but a hired mercenary in the bands that very rich families in my own country employ to guard them and their belongings. But go on and tell us what you have in mind."

"Dingus and I have got a tremendous amount of loot hidden away, Ki," Frank James said. "I haven't figured out how much it adds up to, but there's a lot of it."

"Why, I thought you shared equally with the men in your gang, Mr. James," Jessie said. "How does it happen that you have all this loot hidden?"

"There aren't many people who understand how outlaws work, Miss Starbuck," James replied. "Now, let me ask you something before I go on, and maybe it'll make it easier for you to understand. From what I've learned, you've got a lot of businesses making money for you. That's right, isn't it?"

"Of course." Jessie frowned. "My father was a very successful man, and I inherited the businesses he'd created."

James nodded. "Now tell me, do you take all that money those businesses make, or do you split it up even-steven with those people you hire to run them?"

"Why—of course I don't divide the profits evenly," Jessie answered. "The people who work for the Starbuck enterprises all receive very good wages every week they work. That was something Alex insisted on, paying his employees well; and I've continued to follow his example. But I certainly don't split every penny of the profits with them."

"That's what I figured," the outlaw said.

"Surely you didn't just pay your men a salary!" Ki said.

"No, Ki, that wouldn't've worked at all. When it comes right down to it, though, we didn't do much different from

56

what Miss Starbuck does with her businesses. Dingus and me would split the loot in two parts—half for him and me, and the rest we'd split even-steven with the men in our gang that helped us carry out the plans we'd made."

"Did that satisfy them?" Ki asked.

"Sure it did, Ki," James replied. "Why, the money those boys in our gang got was more than most of them had ever seen in their whole lives, especially when they'd just be starting. And they knew it was our brains that made those jobs work. Every man-jack of our gang knew we'd put in a lot of time and work in coming up with the plans for the jobs they pulled off."

"But some got dissatisfied later?" Ki prompted him.

"Some." James nodded. "But when they'd act up too much, we just didn't pay any mind to them, and we didn't invite them to join up with us on our next job."

"You didn't have the same men in your gang all the time, then?" Jessie asked.

"Oh, my goodness, no, Miss Starbuck," James answered quickly. "There'd always be one or two who'd pull away after a job. And a few who didn't stick with us long got gangs of their own together, like Cole Younger and his brothers." He smiled, shook his head, and went on: "Well, now, when you come down to it, there was enough Youngers to make up a pretty good gang just in the family. But Cole and Bob and the others threw in with us a lot of times on a big job."

"So you and your brother had the first gang?" Jessie asked.

"My goodness, no, Miss Jessie!" James said again, quickly. "We didn't start the gangs at all, even if a lot of folks think we did. There was Doc Bender's outfit up in Wyoming Territory. And Big Nose George, he had him a gang a long time before Dingus and I did. As a matter of

57

fact, Dingus rode with the Big Nose gang before the two of us started out on our own."

"I see." Jessie nodded. Then she went on: "But we're getting away from what we started talking about. You were telling us that you and your brother hid your share of the loot, the half share you took out before dividing with your men."

"Oh, we didn't always take half of what we'd got," the outlaw replied quickly. "After a little job we'd just split up—share and share alike. But when we hit a big take, Dingus and I would take half and then we'd hide away most of it. Buried it, generally, someplace where we knew nobody else could stumble across it. Or maybe, in country where there's a lot of caves, we'd put it in a little one and pile rocks up over the mouth."

"And you know where all of it's hidden?" Jessie asked.

James nodded. "Why, sure."

"And I suppose you have a pretty good idea of how much you have buried or in caves or wherever you hid it?"

"I couldn't tell you to a penny, because on some jobs we'd get a lot of jewelry—diamonds and rubies and pearls and watches and rings and things like that. And sometimes we'd get gold or silver bullion instead of coined money. Why, in a cave just across the Rio Grande we've got something like twenty mulepack loads of silver bullion bars that Dingus and I took in a job down close to Matamoros."

"Make a guess, then," Ki suggested.

Frank James shook his head. "I couldn't even come close, Ki. You see, when Dingus and I would be resting up between jobs and run short of cash, one or the other or maybe both of us would go to the closest stash and get whatever we needed to tide us over till we could set up another job. We didn't keep much count of what we took out."

58

Jessie frowned. "Surely you'd know about how much is left in your hiding-places."

"Well, now, I don't much care to sound like I'm bragging, Miss Starbuck. That's not my style. Jesse likes to, now and again, but he's a lot different from me. If you've just got to know, though, I'd say there's close to a million dollars in all of our stashes put together."

"That's a great deal of money," Jessie said.

"I guess that's right," James agreed. "And like I told you, Dingus and I both feel like we might get pardons if we dug all of it up and gave it to the authorities."

"I don't like to bring up a touchy subject," Ki said, "but do you think the authorities—the ones you'd be asking for a pardon—would give you one if you returned your loot?"

"There's not any way of telling, Ki," James answered. "I figure maybe if somebody like Miss Starbuck was to go along with me when I dug it up, and I was to hand over all of it to her, so she could say I didn't take out any of it, they might believe me and Dingus when we swore to go straight from now on out."

"Suppose they didn't?" Jessie asked. "Suppose they said you'd have to stand trial and serve prison terms for the robberies—and worse, I suppose—that you're charged with now? What would you do?"

"That's a bridge I've been trying not to cross," James said soberly. "And as God's my witness, I don't know what I'd say."

"Can't you make up your mind whether you want to go straight or keep on being an outlaw?" Jessie frowned. "Because if you can't convince me you mean what you've told us about quitting the kind of life you've been following, I don't see that my help would do you a bit of good."

"Oh, I can see that," James replied. He was silent for a moment. Then he went on: "But I'll tell you one thing that's gospel truth, Miss Jessie. Lately, there've been times when I think I've got two sets of brains in my head. One set makes me feel all put-out and sad and sorry about the kind of life I've led up to now. The other set—well, it's something like I'm ready to team up with the devil again, because I feel as mean and ornery as Satan himself."

Chapter 6

Both Jessie and Ki had recognized that Frank James' agonized confession was true. For a moment, the three sat in silence. It was Jessie who spoke first:

"I don't question the honesty of anything you've told us, Mr. James," she said quietly. "But there are still a number of questions in my mind that would need to be answered before I could even consider your suggestion."

"You go ahead and ask me anything that's on your mind," James told her.

"One of the things I'm curious about is why you came here alone. Where's your brother Jesse?"

"He's living back East, Miss Jessie, going by the name of Bob Howard. You see, we split up so folks wouldn't recognize us so quick. Since the Pinkertons got after us, we've had a mite of trouble keeping a jump or two ahead of them."

"Didn't the Pinkerton men bomb one of your hideouts a few years ago?" Ki frowned. "It seems to me I recall hearing that they did."

"Sure as shooting they did, Ki." Frank James nodded. "You know, folks call us James boys outlaws, but there's outlaws on the other side of the law, too. That bomb killed our little step-brother, and it tore our mother's arm off. Dingus and I and a couple of our men were in the house, all right, but our rooms were upstairs, so we didn't get hurt."

"I can sympathize with you about that," Jessie said. Frank James's words had recalled to her mind the day when Alex Starbuck met his death at the hands of the cartel's assassins. "My father was killed in an ambush set up by enemies who wanted to take over his business enterprises. Ki and I fought them for years because of that."

James nodded, then said, "Dingus and me are still fighting ours. Even if we were on the wrong side of the law, what those Pinkertons did put them outside of it, too. Oh, we killed one of them, and shot up another one, but that didn't bring back our baby step-brother, or give our mother a new arm."

"We're getting off the subject again," Jessie reminded him. "I still want to find out more about what you'd expect me to do for you, Mr. James."

"Now, that's real simple to lay out, Miss Starbuck," James replied. "Like I told you, Dingus and I are tired of being on the dodge, the way we've been living most of our lives. And we don't expect to get off scot-free if we give up to the law. We know we've both got bad reputations, and I can't argue that we don't deserve them."

"Your reputations are among the things that make me wonder why you think you can surrender and get pardons or amnesty or whatever it might be," Jessie told the outlaw.

"Oh, we both know that," James agreed. "And we figure we'll have to serve some time. Now I'm already past forty, and Jesse's just a few years younger than me. I've got a nice wife and a boy growing up that I don't see as much of as I'd like to, and Dingus and his wife are raising up a family, too. He wanted to be with them awhile; that's the only reason why he's not here with me right now."

"So you and I—and Ki, of course—would be the ones to unearth this loot you were telling us about and return it." Jessie nodded thoughtfully. "And I'm sure you'd expect me to testify for you at your trial after you surrendered."

"That's about the size of it, Miss Starbuck," James said. "You'd be able to say that I didn't try to make off with what we dug up, and tell how I came to you of my own free will and accord to ask you to go along and make sure I didn't help myself to any of the money or stuff that I'd led you to."

A frown had been growing on Jessie's face while Frank James talked. Now she asked, "Just why did you and your brother choose me as your witness, Mr. James?"

"For a lot of reasons," he replied. "First off, we figure you'd know a lot of pretty high-placed political muckety-mucks that might put in a good word for us when we stand trial."

"It's true that I know a lot of men in politics and finance, and I suppose I could persuade a few to take my word about your good intentions," Jessie agreed after a moment's thought. "But I'd better warn you that they might not be very enthusiastic about doing it. In fact, some would very likely say that they only agreed to testify because I asked them to."

"But if you did ask them, they would?" James asked.

"Quite probably. But the only good reason I could give for asking them is the suggestion that getting you and your brother to give up your lawless ways would save a lot of money and probably quite a few lives. Even then it's not likely that you'd get off completely free. The best you could expect would be a term in prison—perhaps ten years or more."

63

"Dingus and me didn't expect we'd get off scot-free. We figure ten years is about the best we can hope for, with the bad name we've got," Frank replied. "But there's two more real good reasons why we picked you out, Miss Starbuck."

"I'd like to hear them," she said.

"One is that if you're watching me when I go to the stashes where Dingus and I put our loot, and I turned it over to you right then and there, folks would believe you when you said that we were giving back every penny of it and not taking any more for ourselves."

"Yes, if you dug it up without some witnesses, I suppose there would be that kind of suspicion, and talk and speculation," Jessie said thoughtfully.

"And the other reason," Frank James went on, "is that you're one of the richest people in this country—maybe in the world, for all I know. You've got so much money that you don't need any more, so Dingus and me wouldn't have to be worrying about you trying to slip any of the loot we dig up into your own pockets."

In spite of herself, a smile flickered over Jessie's face at the outlaw's frankness. She waited until her voice would not reflect her amusement at the outlaw's very practical worry. Then she said, "I think all your reasons make good sense, Mr. James."

"You'll help us, then?" he asked, not even trying to hide the eagerness in his voice.

"I'm not going to say yes or no right this minute," she told him. "But I'll talk with Ki, and if I decide to consider your request, we'll want to know where we'd be going and what kind of trouble we might run into. Suppose you stroll around the ranch for a while, and give me and Ki a chance to talk."

"Why, sure," James replied. "I'll be glad to do that. I'll

64

use the time to learn a little bit about how you run the Circle Star. It'll likely be helpful if we ever get free. I don't suppose you know it, but Dingus and me have a few little spreads of our own where we spend our time between jobs. None of them's as big or fancy as this place of yours, of course."

"Not that it's any of my business," Ki said, "and I'll understand if you don't feel like answering me, but, except for the ranch you were coming from in Mexico, do you use any of the others for hideouts when the law's on your trail?"

Without hesitating, James replied, "Sure we do. That's why we bought them in the first place. Our real names don't show on the deeds, of course, and there's nobody except family who knows about them. Oh, the Youngers know, Cole and his brothers, but they're the same as family to Dingus and me."

Jessie asked, "If I should agree to help you, Mr. James, would we be able to use one of your other places as—well, a base of operations while we're collecting the loot you've got hidden away?"

James was silent for a long minute. Then he said, "I'd have to think about that, Miss Starbuck. The trouble is, none of our other places is close to where we'd be going to collect the money and stuff that we'd be after."

"You're a badly wanted man, Mr. James." She frowned. "And from what you've just said, we'd have to do a lot of traveling to get to all the places where you've hidden your loot. What would happen if someone recognized you while we were going from one place to another?"

"I've thought about that, too," James replied. "But none of the places we'd be going to is what you'd call crowded. Besides that, anybody who'd recognize me would most likely be an outlaw, too, and they sure wouldn't give me away."

"But there are "Wanted" posters with your pictures on them all over the country," Ki put in.

"I'll grant you that," James agreed. "But you're looking at me right now. Do I look like the pictures on those posters?"

"No, I'd have to say you don't," Ki replied.

"All those pictures were drawn by men who've never seen me or Dingus," James went on. "And we sure don't go around getting our tintypes made."

Jessie nodded and said, "I can understand that. Well, Mr. James, you've made a very interesting request, but it's one I'll have to think about. And I'll want to talk to Ki, too. I won't take a long time to decide. While you're waiting, please make yourself at home."

Nodding, the outlaw left the room, and a moment later Jessie and Ki heard the latch on the big front door click shut. Jessie turned to Ki, her eyebrows raised inquiringly.

"What do you think, Ki?" she asked.

"I'm not really sure." He frowned. "Of course, neither of us had any idea what sort of a proposal he was going to make, and I suppose I'm still a little bit surprised to find that a man with the reputation the James brothers have can be as soft-spoken as Frank James seems to be."

"I doubt that we'd find him that polite if he was holding us up," Jessie said. "We already know what an efficient gunfighter he is after watching him do away with those rustlers. And I'm not sure that I want to get mixed up in this business he's asked us to help him with."

"That's a decision only you can make, Jessie," Ki told her.

Jessie nodded absently. Then, talking to herself as much

as to Ki, she went on: "I suppose that I'd be doing a service to the public—especially those who ride trains or have money in a bank—if I did something that would help stop the James brothers from pulling off any more robberies."

"Of course you would," Ki agreed. "I'd say the main thing you have to decide is whether you want to get caught up in any sort of dealings with the James brothers. You know how gossip grows as it travels. The next rumor might be that you've lost or spent all the money you inherited from Alex, and joined the James brothers to make a new fortune."

"I don't really think that anybody would accuse me of needing to steal, Ki." Jessie smiled. "One of my problems is that too many people know I'm well-off."

"I know that, Jessie, and the public knows it as well. But most people seem anxious to believe any sort of wild rumor or twisted-up yarn."

"You know, Ki," Jessie went on, her voice very sober now, "there's only one thing that kept me from agreeing at once to give Frank James the help he's asking for. I don't like the idea of handling stolen money. If there was any way I could be sure that he and his brother would go straight, I'd be inclined to help them. But I'm afraid they've been outlaws too long to change their ways, in spite of their good intentions."

"Well, it's your decision to make," Ki said. "And I think the best thing I can do to help you right now is go take care of the chores that I've been neglecting and let you think your way through this."

"I suppose that's the best thing you can do, Ki," she said. "It's my problem, and it's up to me to solve it. We'll talk with Frank James again after supper."

* * *

"Well, Miss Jessie, you were mighty quiet all the time we were eating supper," Frank James said as they stood up from the dinner table. "Do you still need some time to think about what I asked you, or have you decided now?"

"I've decided on my answer," Jessie told him. "And I'm afraid there isn't any way I can sugar-coat it."

"Which means you're going to say no, I take it?" James asked. His voice was flat and his face showed no emotion.

Jessie nodded and said, "I can't help you return the stolen money, Mr. James. I understand why you'd want someone who isn't connected with making laws or enforcing them, or who holds political office, to act as a witness for you, but if I stood up on your side I'd seem to be endorsing the crimes you and your brother have committed in the past. I can't endorse robbery and murder."

"I'm sure sorry to hear you say that, Miss Jessie," James said. His voice did not reflect sorrow or any other emotion. It was flat and expressionless and carried no tone of defeat. He went on, "But I guess I know why you'd feel like you do."

"I'm sorry I had to refuse you," Jessie told him. "But I'm sure that you and your brother can find someone else to be your witness."

"Oh, I imagine we will." James nodded. He glanced around the room and went on, "You've got a real nice place here, Miss Jessie. I appreciate you putting me up and all that, but our business is over now, and Dingus is going to be looking for me back in Saint Joe, so I'll be riding on in the morning."

"You're welcome to stay longer if you need more rest," Jessie offered.

Shaking his head, James said, "Thanks kindly, but I'm used to hard riding. And the sooner I start the sooner I'll get to where I'm heading. Now I'll bid you good evening, Miss Jessie. And you, too, Ki."

After Frank James had disappeared upstairs, Ki said, "He certainly took your refusal like a man, Jessie."

"I'd never question the manhood of either one of the James brothers, even if I don't like the way they've displayed it," Jessie replied. "And in one way, I'm sorry I felt that I had to refuse to be their witness. In spite of his reputation, Frank James seems to be a straightforward sort of man."

"He does, at that," Ki agreed. "But if I'd been in your place, I suppose I'd have come up with the same answer, Jessie. And now that the question's been answered, I think I'll follow our guest's example and go to bed early."

"Good night, then, Ki," Jessie replied. "I'm going to bed soon, but I'm going to sit here and think a few minutes."

As was his habit, Ki rose early the next morning. Dawn was just graying the eastern sky when he glanced out the window of his bedroom. The bunkhouse windows were dark, but even in the vague, wavering gray light that preceded sunup he could see that the horses used by the ranch hands were already gone from the big pole corral that stood a short distance past the bunkhouse.

Only Ki's horse and the sorrel gelding ridden by Frank James were in the big corral. In the small corral at the end, Sun was standing. Directly across the cleared area that separated it from the main house, lights showed in the cookhouse. Ki walked across the clear space and went inside. Gimpy, back on his old job after a prolonged spree, looked up from the big cast-iron range that took up most of one end of the long narrow building.

"If you're here to take the breakfast grub over to the

69

main house, you got here a mite too soon," Gimpy said. "Because if that's what you're after, you'll have to wait till I sizzle up some fresh flapjacks."

"I'm the only one up so far," Ki told him. "I'll have some coffee and a biscuit or two, if the hands left any."

"I always cook enough for you and Miss Jessie to have what you want, Ki," Gimpy replied. "And like now, when somebody's visiting, I put in extra flour when I mix the dough." He filled a coffee cup from the big graniteware pot, and as he handed it to Ki he dropped his voice a bit to ask, "Is that fellow staying here really Jesse James' brother, Ki? Seems like he's all the hands have talked about since you and Miss Jessie rode in with him yesterday evening."

Ki nodded. "He's Frank James. At least he claims to be, and Jessie and I both think he's telling the truth."

"That's what Cord claims, too," Gimpy said. "Is he going to be around awhile?"

"He told us last night that he'll be moving on today," Ki replied. "And I'm sure he meant it."

"If he knows what's good for him, he'll get out fast," the grizzled old cook said without interrupting his preparations at the range. "Some of the boys was talking while they ate breakfast about how much reward money's posted on him. It wouldn't surprise me none if one or two of 'em takes after him when he leaves."

"Let me know if you hear any more talk like that, and I'll advise them not to try taking him," Ki said. "He's deadly with a gun, and he doesn't hesitate to use one."

"I'll pass the word along if I get the chance," Gimpy replied. He fell silent for a moment while he stacked the pancakes on a big platter and added a smaller platter of bacon to the breakfast tray. Then he went on: "But I figure the hands are likely all blow and no go. Anyways, they

70

won't be back till close to sundown, and if you're right about him leaving, he'll be long gone before then."

"You're probably right," Ki agreed as he picked up the tray and turned to start back to the main house. "But pass the word along to them, even if Frank James does leave this morning."

Back at the main house, Ki kindled a fire in the small range in the kitchen and put on a pot of coffee. He went into the dining room and was setting the table for breakfast when Frank James came in.

"I hope you don't mind me nosing around so early," James said. "But I'm used to getting up and moving as soon as there's enough light to see by."

"I can understand that," Ki told the outlaw. "Jessie and I have the same habit. I'm surprised that she's not up yet."

"I didn't hear anyone stirring upstairs." James frowned. "But I'd like to get started as soon as I can, and I don't want to leave without thanking Miss Jessie again."

"Jessie wouldn't want you to leave without any breakfast," Ki said. "Neither do I, for that matter. Why don't you sit down? I'll go up and see what's keeping Jessie."

Mounting the stairs in quick, nimble strides, Ki listened for a moment outside the door of Jessie's bedroom. When he heard no sounds of her moving around inside, he tapped lightly on the door with his fingertips and called her name. When he got no response, he waited, listening for sounds of movement.

Frowning now, Ki rapped sharply with his knuckles. When his call was not answered, he opened the door and looked inside. Jessie's bed was untouched, showing that it had not been slept in. And Jessie was not in the room.

A morning breeze blew one of the lacy window curtains and started it rippling. Ki stepped to the window. Its glass pane had been shattered, and when he glanced out he saw a pole-ladder, a tree-trunk notched to make footholds, lying on the ground near the wall. Though seeing the ladder was all that Ki really needed, he glanced at the windowsill to confirm the conclusion that was setting alarm-bells ringing in his mind. The mark where the ladder had rested on the windowsill was very plain to his eyes. He huried downstairs.

"Jessie's been kidnapped," he told Frank James. "And I hope your men didn't have anything to do with it or—"

"Hold on, Ki!" James broke in. "Dammit, I don't mind being called an outlaw, but I haven't got a gang with me down here; my men are all back East. And besides, I might be an outlaw, but I'm sure not as bad a one as you're thinking right now! Miss Jessie was real nice to me, and I wouldn't lift a finger to harm her!"

Ki heard truth in the outlaw's words and realized instantly what must have happened. He said, "Those outlaws from Mexico! They've kidnapped her for revenge!"

Frank James nodded. His blue eyes were colder than ever. "Yes, that's likely. Let's go outside and see what we can find. I guess you'll know a little bit about reading ground-signs."

"Of course I do," Ki replied. He was icily calm now. He went on: "Enough to follow them and get Jessie out of their hands."

"I figured that's what you'd say." James nodded. "And if you figure to set out and follow them, I hope you won't object to my company, because whether you like it or not, I'm riding with you!"

Chapter 7

For a moment Ki stared at the outlaw. His first thought was to refuse Frank James's help. Then his common sense returned.

"You're sure you want to?" he asked. "After Jessie refused to help you?"

"I don't need a long time to make up my mind about what I've got to do, Ki," James replied. "Miss Jessie doesn't, either. Her not beating around the bush, but coming right out with the truth is one of the things I like about her. I'm riding with you, and I'll thank you if you don't try to make me change my mind."

Ki nodded. "I won't try. Let's take a look at the ground under Jessie's window. We ought to find some tracks there that will give us an idea."

On the unbroken soil below the window of Jessie's room, there was the deep oval imprint five or six feet from the wall. It had been made by the improvised scaling-ladder used by the kidnappers, and was surrounded by a mixture of fresh bootprints.

"These were made by smaller, narrower boots than you see on this side of the border," Ki said after he'd looked at them for a moment. "And I'd say there were three of them."

"They didn't go to any trouble to hide 'em, either," James said. He shook his head. "No wonder you caught up so easy with the ones that stole your steers. Why, my boys could give them high, low, and jack and take the game before the deck was halfway played out."

"We shouldn't have any trouble picking up their trail," Ki went on. "I've got to take care of two things before we go. I'll have to tell the foreman what's happened and then get my saddlebags and my *shuriken* from the main house."

"You lost me with that last one," James said. "What's a *shuriken*? Some kind of knife? I know it's not a gun, or I'd have run into it at some time or other."

"I suppose you'd have to call them knives without handles," Ki replied. "They're throwing-blades. I can use them at quite a distance, and they're quieter than a gun. They don't let off a flash of muzzle-blast in the dark to give away my position, either."

"Get whatever you need," James said. "And I'd be real obliged if you'll step into the room where I slept last night and pick up my rifle and saddlebags, too. I'll get over to the corral and start saddling up."

Ki needed very little time to race upstairs and pick up their gear, since neither he nor Frank James had unpacked their saddlebags the previous evening. He stopped at the bunkhouse and gave Rance Sanders an abbreviated outline of what was going on, then took off at a run to the corral. Frank James was tightening the girth on his dapple. Ki dropped the outlaw's saddlebags and rifle beside the horse and got busy saddling the sturdy roan gelding that he'd gotten used to.

James finished getting his dapple ready first, and while Ki was fitting the headstall on his pony, took his second revolver out of one side of his saddlebags and threaded his belt through the slots in the holster. He also took out a handful of shells for the rifle and dropped them in one pocket of his coat. Then he dipped into the bag for spare pistol cartridges, putting them in the opposite coat pocket.

He mounted then, and waited for Ki to get into his saddle before saying, "You know the country here better than I do, Ki. You ride lead and I'll stay on your flank."

"If we're right about who kidnapped Jessie, we can catch up with them just by backtracking that herd we drove in yesterday," Ki said. "And I can't think right now of anybody else who'd have had a reason to take her."

"You'd know about Miss Jessie's affairs a lot better than I would," James said. "But that's my bet, too. I know that if somebody cut down eight of my men and ruined a job I'd planned, I'd try to even up the score."

"We'll know as soon as we hit the boundary fence," Ki went on. "The hoofprints they left ought to lead us to where it's been cut again."

"We'll ride, then," Frank James said. "You take the lead, and I'll be with you all the way."

Ki and the outlaw mounted in silence and started across the range. As they rode, Ki turned to his companion and said, "Those men can't have more than a five- or six-hour start on us. They wouldn't've taken Jessie until after all the lamps were out and the bunkhouse and the house were both quiet."

"If I know outlaws' ways, which I guess I do, they'd have hit about three or four o'clock this morning," James said. "And their horses sure won't be fresh for the ride back. I'd say that all we've got to do is push right along. Chances are we'll catch 'em a long time before they get anywhere close to the Rio Grande."

Frank James's prediction proved accurate. The sun was still high in the western sky when they topped a long pull up a gentle slope and reached the rim of a wide, shallow valley. The depression below them was almost circular in shape, the same shape that Ki had seen many times in his native Japan; he recognized it at once as being the crater of a long-dead volcano. Like most of the arid country in that section of Texas, the valley supported only sparse vegetation; thin-stemmed ocotillo and some clumps of prickly pear and a few small stretches of mesquite-brush rose above the knee-high grass that rippled gently across it in the languid breeze.

Six or seven miles away, three riders were crossing the valley floor, making slow progress toward the slanting trail that zigzagged back and forth as it wound up the opposite side of the valley. Though Ki and his companion could not make out small details at such a distance, they could see that one of the horses was carrying double.

"That's them all right, Ki," James said as they watched the little group ahead. "All we've got to do now is figure out a way to circle around ahead of 'em and jump 'em before they can hurt Miss Jessie."

"It's easier to talk about it than it'll be to do it, in this open country." Ki frowned. "We can move faster than they're able to, but there's not much cover we can use to get close to them."

"That's not exactly what I had in mind," James said.

"Maybe you'd better explain, then," Ki suggested.

"With the daylight we've got left, we'll have plenty of time to circle around ahead of them and let them come to us."

"Where we will take them by surprise." Ki nodded.

"The first thing I learned when I started studying *ninjitsu* was the value of a sudden, unexpected attack."

"I don't know what this *ninjitsu* you're talking about amounts to," James broke in. "But I'm talking outlaw language now." He glanced up at the sun and went on: "We've got maybe three more hours of daylight left. If we cut a wide loop around the side of this valley, and take off cross-country at a slant toward the trail, we can cut back then and get in front of those Mexican bandits before dark."

"But even if we attack them from the front, Jessie will still be in danger!" Ki protested.

"Just keep listening to me, Ki," Frank James said. He went on: "Those fellows are watching for somebody to come at 'em from behind, and they know what the trail's like ahead of them, so they won't be paying all that much attention to what's in front of 'em. And I can see a way to get Miss Jessie away from them, too. I'd sure be mad at myself if I let that little lady get hurt."

"If we can free Jessie before they have a chance to harm her I don't suppose you care any more than I do what happens to the men who kidnapped her," Ki said. "I've been trying to figure out a way to do it, but in this open country—"

"This *ninjitsu* thing you've talked about," James broke in, "does it stretch to hiding out and jumping up all of a sudden where nobody expects you to be, the way I've heard my grandpa tell about the way redskins used to do?"

"Of course." Ki nodded.

"And you're pretty good at it, I expect?"

"I've spent a long time learning *ninjitsu* from some of the great masters in my homeland," Ki said, nodding. "What is it you have in mind for me to do?"

"If our horses hold out, we'll be in front of the Mexicans in another half-hour or so, if we cut a shuck around this valley," James replied thoughtfully. "Now, when we find a place where the land lays just right, suppose I ride on ahead of you for maybe a quarter of a mile or so while you find a stand of brush big enough to hide you and your horse in. I'll keep an eye on you and see where you've holed up. Then you just get into the brush and wait."

"When do you plan to start shooting?" Ki asked.

"I'm coming to that. First off, I'll limp my horse a bit, so they'll think he's gone lame," James replied.

"You've trained him to do that?"

"Sure. When you're on the owl-hoot trail you've got to learn all the tricks going, and make up a few new ones as you go along, Ki. Now, I'll hold back as long as I can, and when they're as close to you as they're likely to get, I'll start throwing lead. That's when you jump out and grab Miss Jessie."

Ki was beginning to see how the James brothers had survived for so many years as outlaws. He asked, "You're not going to shoot at the man who's got Jessie on his horse, I hope?"

"You ought to know I won't!" James replied. "All I'm going to do is get their minds off her. You're sure you can jump up from behind and grab her off that fellow's horse if they get close to you?"

"Of course," Ki said. "And I can take care of the man who's carrying her. I'll sink a *shuriken* into his back as soon as I get close enough."

"Then I'll guarantee to keep the other two so busy they won't have a chance to give you any trouble," James promised. "That's how we'll handle it, then, when we get back close to that trail they're on. It might not be the best scheme in the world, but it's the only one I can come up with."

"It sounds all right to me," Ki said. "Even if it is a little bit chancy."

"Oh, it's not all that farfetched," Frank James told him. "I tumbled to it when I was with old Quantrill, and he used it to take Clell Miller away from a squad of blue-coats. Then Dingus and me pulled the Quantrill stunt again, back in Missouri when we had to get Cole Younger away from a posse that was taking him to jail."

"Outlaw tactics and *ninjitsu* tactics have a lot in common," Ki said, smiling. "I understand your plan perfectly. Let's not waste any more time talking about it."

"Of course, there's not any guarantee that the two of us can pull it off as smooth."

Ki nodded. "I understand." He went on: "You keep looking for the right place when we get back to the trail those men with Jessie are taking. I'll try to keep up with you when we start."

Left to his own devices, Ki might have adopted exactly the same tactics the outlaw had proposed, but he'd recognized that James had an urgent need to be a leader. As they'd started out to pursue the outlaws and free Jessie, Ki had resolved to let his companion have as free a hand as possible. During the long series of battles which he and Jessie had fought in demolishing the cartel, Ki had also discovered that even the best plans must be flexible enough to allow for changes made necessary by unexpected developments. The outlaw tactics outlined by Frank James might well have been those Ki himself would have evolved.

In unspoken accord, Ki and James reined their horses off the trail and dropped behind the rim of the wide, shallow valley through which Jessie's captors were now traveling. Hidden from the Mexican bandits, Frank James spurred his mount mercilessly, as though he was leading his band in a wild ride to escape a sheriff's posse. He soon drew ahead of Ki as they rode in a half-circle, skirting the rim of the big wide valley.

Ki managed to keep his companion in sight, though the tough little range-hardened gelding was forced to take two strides to each one of the big dapple James was riding. The arid open country, high summer-browned prairie grasses broken only by the occasional clumps of heavier vegetation that had to be skirted, might have been tailored to exactly the kind of all-out galloping the two horses were now doing. The horses responded, but were panting heavily when Frank James at last reined in and waited for Ki to catch up with him.

"We've got a ways to go yet," the outlaw said. "But those Mexicans can't make as good time riding up-slope out of that hollow as they have on level ground. If I've judged rightly, they'll be riding up-slope about now, and that hollow gets a mite steeper toward the top of it."

"We'll make it in time," Ki said calmly. While he'd been riding he'd mentally ticked off the minutes, gauging their own progress against that of Jessie's captors. "How wide do you want to swing before we angle back toward the trail?"

"I've been watching the way the land lays, Ki. Another two or three miles and we can start cutting back."

James turned his horse and they spurred ahead. Ki was not prepared for the burst of speed the dapple showed. It spurted forward and pulled away from him at once, and was in the lead by a hundred yards before Ki's ranch-trained mount could close most of the gap between them. At last he gave up trying to catch up with James and managed to keep the same distance between them as they galloped at a long slant around the valley's rim.

They'd covered almost two miles when James turned in

his saddle and pointed ahead. Ki looked in the direction his companion was indicating and saw the trail that led from the crater's rim, zigzagging down the slope.

"That's the kind of trail that's made just for us," he said. "They'll be going slow and chances are they won't be watching too far ahead. Tether your pony and pick out your spot, Ki. I'll wait till you've got settled into it, then I'll move down and find a good curve in the trail below you. After you've got Jessie safe, I'll take care of the rest."

Ki dismounted and began zigzagging up the steep slope. He watched the terrain closely, and after he'd covered about a third of the distance, he found a cluster of boulders where he and Jessie could hide. He marked its location, then started looking for a suitable position close to the trail. On the broken ground of the extinct volcano's flank, a hiding place was not too hard to discover. A thick clump of ocotillo rose only a few yards away from a short straight stretch of the trail, its red flowers sprouting profusely to screen the ground behind it. Ki moved into position and hunkered down to wait.

Surprisingly little time passed before the hooves of the men who'd kidnapped Jessie grated on the hard ground. A few more moments and he could hear their voices:

"*Estás pensando de esta noche, Julio?*" one of them asked.

"*Tu sabes que sí, compañero,*" one of his companions answered. "*Esta noche tendremos la mujer solamente para nosotros!*"

"*Cuidado, amigos!*" the third man put in. "*No queremos aburella antes de los otros acasala!*"

Their loud laughter at the crude joke lasted until the three had passed Ki's hiding-place. As soon as the sound of their horses' hooves grating on the hard soil of the path showed that the trio had passed beyond his hiding-place,

Ki moved. Dropping flat, he wriggled and crawled through the shielding growth of ocotilla, his eyes flicking from one of the outlaws to another as he slid a *shuriken* from his vest pocket.

Jessie was riding astride the horse in front of the saddle of the man in the center of the trio. Her hands were bound behind her and a rope circling her neck was looped around the saddle-horn. Ki saw at once that he'd be taking a risk of failing in his mission unless he could attack the man Jessie was riding with. He slipped another *shuriken* out of his pocket and gauged the distance of his throw with the quick certainty that came from long experience. Then he sent one of the star-shaped blades with its razor-keen points sailing through the air.

True to Ki's aim, the *shuriken* sliced into the rump of the horse ridden by the man at the back of the line. The wounded horse leaped forward, screaming. Its leap carried it into a collision with the horse on which Jessie was riding with her captor, and sent horse and riders veering off the narrow trail.

In the distance ahead, Frank James' rifle cracked. The man on the lead horse threw his arms wide, dropping the reins as he toppled slowly forward.

Meanwhile, Ki had taken advantage of the clear target now offered by the man on whose horse Jessie was riding. Before the echoes of Frank James's shot died away, he whirled the second *shuriken*. Like the first blade, the second found its target. The finely-honed points of Ki's throwing-blade penetrated the rider's neck an inch above his shoulder.

With a howl of pain the rider rose in his stirrups, one arm hanging limp, his other hand clawing at the *shuriken,* which was still lodged in his shoulder near the base of his neck.

Ki slid a third *shuriken* from his pocket. This time he threw to kill. The course of the second throwing-blade took it home, into the man's neck, above the first, severing his sternal muscles and femoral artery. A single gargling gasp escaped his throat before he fell to the ground in a limp sprawl.

Even before the second bullet from James' rifle dropped the rider whose horse Ki had wounded, Jessie had understood what was happening. She bent low over the neck of the horse to present the smallest possible target. Then, unable to use her hands, she began kicking the animal's chest and shoulders. The tattoo of her heels on its chest confused the animal, it had not been trained to react to a command of that sort. The horse stopped short, then began wheeling in the underbrush beside the trail.

Before the animal's panicked antics could dislodge Jessie from her precarious position, Ki reached her side. A single leap and a mid-air twist put him in the saddle behind Jessie. He wrapped an arm around her and held her in place while with his free hand he worked at the knots that bound her wrists until she could slip her hands free.

"I'm all right now, Ki," she said. "I guess that was Frank James shooting, ahead of us?"

"Yes. Just hold on. We'll be down the slope where to he is in a minute or two."

Ki broke off as Frank James' rifle cracked again. By now the horse carrying Jessie and Ki was plunging down the slope. Ki did the best he could to keep it moving straight ahead, past the riderless horses of Jessie's kidnappers. They'd covered only fifty or sixty yards when they saw James riding toward them. Ki had found the reins by now, and pulled up the plunging steed that was carrying him and Jessie.

"Looks like you came through all right," James remarked, his voice as casual as though he was bidding them good morning.

"I'm fine," Jessie replied. "And I'm sure Ki is, too."

"Of course I am," Ki told them. Looking at James, he added, "Your plan was a very good one."

"I can't take all that much credit," the outlaw said. "But I'm sure glad it worked. Give me a minute to tend to those loose horses, and we can start back to your ranch, Miss Jessie."

"But the dead men—" Jessie began.

"Don't worry your head about them. When they don't show up at wherever their bunch is hid out, somebody'll come looking for them," James told her. Before she could reply, he'd reined his dapple around and was riding up the slope.

Chapter 8

As the outlaw disappeared into the brush, Jessie turned to Ki and asked, "Did you ask him to join you in coming after me?"

"No. He was ready to do that the minute I told you you were gone. And how in the world did those bandits manage to capture you without raising an alarm?"

"They were hidden in my room, waiting for me when I went upstairs," she replied. "I started to close the door and one of them grabbed me from behind it, another one clamped his hand over my mouth and the third one took hold of my feet. They had me gagged and tied up within— well, it only seemed like a few seconds, but I'm sure it took a bit longer."

"I can guess the rest from what I saw," Ki said, nodding. "They lowered you down that ladder they'd made and carried you to wherever their horses were waiting."

"So you didn't know I was gone until I didn't come down to breakfast?"

"I went upstairs to call you because Frank James was getting ready to leave. He wanted to thank you and—"

"Thank me?" Jessie broke in. "After what he'd done to help us with those rustlers, and after I refused to give him the help he asked me for? Even after I'd turned him down, he was ready to help me a second time?"

"Your refusal didn't seem to bother him," Ki told her. "And he's certainly helped me in freeing you. When I told him you'd been kidnapped, his first thought was to ride after you. I didn't ask him to come with me, Jessie. He was ready to start out to try to find you the minute I told him what had happened."

Jessie was silent for a moment. Then she said thoughtfully, "I'm afraid I've been misjudging Frank James, Ki."

"Don't be too sure," Ki cautioned. "We talked a bit while we were tracking those men who kidnapped you. He doesn't even try to hide the fact that he's an outlaw and that he shoots first and asks questions afterward."

"So do a number of the lawmen we've run into, Ki," Jessie reminded him. "And you and I have had to do the same thing at times to keep from being murdered by one of those hired killers the cartel sent out to get rid of us."

"That was—"

"I know," Jessie broke in. "That was different. Of course it was. Just the same, Frank James fought those rustlers with us the other day, and even after I'd refused to help him, you've just said that he was ready to help me the minute he heard about what had happened this time."

"You think he's serious about wanting to get away from his outlaw life, then?"

"Oh, I've never doubted that, Ki. If he hadn't been serious he'd never have come looking for me. And now I can't let my refusal stand. When he comes back, I'm going to tell him I've changed my mind."

"Are you saying that you don't have any record of where all the money you and your brother want to return is hidden?" Jessie asked Frank James as she pushed her dinner plate away and picked up her coffee cup.

Jessie, Ki, and Frank James were sitting at the dinner table in the main house at the ranch. They'd returned to the Circle Star late the previous evening, all three of them bone-weary, and had slept and rested most of the day.

Now Jessie went on: "When we were talking yesterday on the way back, I mentioned that I'd want to know how long it's going to take us to gather up the money you want to return."

"Now don't start worrying, Miss Jessie," James said. "I told you then I'd try to figure it out."

Jessie nodded. Then she said, "I haven't mentioned before what I have on my mind right now, Mr. James, but I'd better warn you of something before we start."

"What's that, Miss Jessie?" he asked.

"If I'm going to be your—well, go-between, I suppose you'd call it, in returning the loot you and your brother have hidden away, I'll expect you to be absolutely honest with me. I don't need to remind you that I'm staking my reputation on what you tell me is true."

"When I give my word to somebody, I don't go back on it, Miss Jessie," Frank James replied very soberly. "I've got a pretty good idea of the kind of fix you could get into if I lied to you. I'd be right unthankful anyhow, if I did a sorry thing like that."

There was a ring of sincerity in his voice that convinced Jessie. She nodded and went on: "I'll take your word, then. Now, let's get on with our job."

"It's a mite hard to get started." James frowned. "Because Dingus and I have got a lot of what we call stashes."

"Yes, I've heard the term before," Jessie said, nodding. "But go on, Mr. James. I didn't mean to interrupt you."

"I don't intend to try to hide anything from you," James

continued. "Especially after you've said you'd changed your mind about helping us."

"But there must be a lot of places where you've hidden this money you want to return!" she protested.

"Sure. And like I said, they're pretty well scattered out. We've put away a right good-sized amount."

"I'm sure you have. For almost as long as I can remember, I've been hearing about the banks you and your brother's gang robbed, and the trains you've held up."

"Well, now, a lot of that's lies the Pinkertons have begun to spread, trying to make our men and their kinfolks jealous, to get them to turn us in."

"I've heard the same stories Jessie has, I'm sure," Ki told the outlaw.

"So has everybody, Ki. A lot of them are just outright lies and the Pinkertons spread some of them around. But don't either you or Miss Jessie worry about me not being able to lead you to the places where we've got loot tucked away. I've got a real good memory, and the location of every place where we hid anything is safe in my mind. And Dingus' memory's just as good as mine is."

"Aren't you afraid you'll forget some of the hiding places you've used?" She frowned.

"Not likely," James replied. "Not after all the trouble we took to hide it."

"And doesn't your brother have a list, either?" Ki asked.

James shook his head. "He remembers, just the same way I do. If you haven't noticed it already, outlaws aren't like other folks, Ki, not if they expect to last very long. You can't run the risk of writing stuff down, like where you've got hideouts or where you go to find a friend who'll take you in and not ask any questions, friends who'll forget

88

you're there if the law or the Pinkertons come asking questions."

Ki nodded. "If I'm right, what you're saying is that there's nobody you can trust."

"Oh, there's a few," James said. "But not all that many. No, Ki, Dingus and I have been lucky. Our kinfolks are still on our side, and there's others who stand by us. That's more than some outlaws I know of can say."

"Then do I understand that you don't intend to give us a list of the places where you have loot hidden?" Jessie asked.

The outlaw nodded. "Right as rain, Miss Jessie. I never was much to write down something in my own hand that could be brought up and shown as evidence in court. But I'll tell you what I will do. If it'll ease your mind any, I'll sit down with you, or with you and Ki both, and tell you how much we've got here and there."

"I'm not interested in how much you have in your hiding-places, Mr. James," Jessie said. "But to save doubling back, I'd like to know where they're located so that we can make the best use of our time traveling to them, so we won't be running all over the country in a lot of zigzags."

"That makes sense," James agreed. "But it won't bother me a bit to tell you where and how much both, now that you're on my side in helping me and Dingus get squared up with the law."

"Would you object if I write down the places we'll have to go?" she asked. "Nobody will see it but you and Ki and me."

"I don't see that it'd do a bit of harm," James agreed.

"Let's move into the study, then," Jessie suggested. "You tell me the places we have to go; I'll jot them down."

Reseated in the study, Jessie at the desk her father had

used, Ki and Frank James in easy chairs, Jessie nodded to James and told him to go ahead with his list.

"I'm going to have to tell you all this by the calendar instead of by the places, Miss Jessie," the outlaw told her. "Because that's how I remember them."

Jessie nodded. "Any way that you choose. I can make up a travel list, as long as I know where we'll be going."

"Well, let's see." James frowned. "The first big job that Dingus and I pulled was in 'sixty-six, at Liberty, Missouri. That's just a little bit east out of Kansas City. We got fifty-eight thousand dollars from the bank there. All but about eight thousand of it was in gold, so we kept the paper money and hid the rest in a little rock cave out east of town. Then we covered up the entrance and went home."

"That was a long time ago," Ki said while Jessie was writing. "Do you really think the money will still be there?"

"Oh, I'd be right surprised if it's not, Ki," James replied. "It's a big rock outcrop, and the folks that live close to it are farmers. They don't pay attention to any land they can't plow up. Now, in 'sixty-seven we held up the bank in Savannah—that's in Missouri, too, about twelve miles north of Saint Joe. We did the same thing with what we got there—kept the shinplasters and hid the gold. I'd say there's maybe thirty thousand dollars tucked away in a bluff that rises out of the Missouri River east of Mound City."

"Above high-water line, I suppose?" Ki asked.

"Sure." James nodded. "We don't hide money in places that aren't safe, Ki. Then in 'sixty-eight, after we'd moved south a ways, we got close to twenty-thousand dollars out of a bank in Russelville, Kentucky. That's just a little ways above the Tennessee line, Miss Jessie, sort of north from Nashville. There was a big plantation house there that got burned out somehow, so we put ten thousand dollars in gold in the old root cellar and covered it good with dirt."

"Do you think you can find a place like that again, after so many years?" Jessie asked, looking up from her note-taking.

"I'd imagine I can take you to it without any trouble," the outlaw answered. "I've got some markers to go by and they're sure to be around when we get there."

When Jessie nodded and resumed writing, James went on: "We went traveling after that bank job, Dingus and me. He sailed down to Panama and went overland to catch another ship up to California, and I took the train there. I don't like sailing all that much, you see. We knocked around out West, mostly in California, looking at what was left of the gold diggings. Then we tried Nevada, but we hadn't much more than got there before we got into a shooting scrape over a poker hand and had to get out pretty fast."

"So you didn't hide anything while you were in California or Nevada?" Jessie asked.

"We didn't have all that much to hide," Frank James admitted. "It was winter, so we swung south and came back by way of El Paso. We sat in on a poker game there and that's how we won our ranch down in Mexico."

"And you're sure that you didn't have anything left over to hide away?" Jessie persisted.

"We didn't have much except traveling money when we crossed the border and set out to look at the ranch we'd won. Then on the way there we ran across a mule train loaded with silver bars. Since we were so short and it wasn't any real trouble, we held it up. There's about two hundred thousand dollars' worth of those bars buried on the ranch right now."

"That's a pretty heavy load," Jessie commented.

"Right heavy," James agreed. "We worked like slaves getting those bars buried. Dingus and I intended to stay down in Mexico for a long time, maybe settle there."

"Do you have any objection to telling me why you changed your minds?" Jessie asked.

"Not a one," James said. "Dingus and I went to Monterrey, just to get a look at it if we had to hide out in Mexico again. We were having a pretty good time when a fellow started making fun of the way I was dancing. He didn't like some of the things I said back to him, so he tried to draw and I had to shoot him. Then it turned out that he had a lot of rich kinfolks, and they had a better inside track with the governor than we did, so we hightailed it back north of the border."

"How long ago was that?" Jessie asked.

"Close to ten years ago. We never did run the ranch ourselves. The old fellow we won it from had a good *capataz* that did all the work. We just left the ranch up to him and hightailed it back home. But when Dingus and me decided we'd better split up for a while, I took a notion to go look at the place again and make sure the silver was still there."

"Then you were on your way to your ranch when you stopped to help Jessie and me the other day?" Ki asked.

James nodded. "I sure was, Ki. I was on my way to the border when I ran into you and Miss Jessie and that gang."

"You're not even sure the silver bars are still there, then?" Jessie frowned.

"I'd be mighty surprised if they'd been uncovered, Miss Jessie. Dingus and I learned how to hide things. I'd bet it's all still there, just where we hid it."

"Then let's go back to the other caches," Jessie suggested.

"Whatever you say," James agreed. He thought for a

moment and went on: "We'd brought part of that silver with us, and most of it went to buy a ranch here in Texas, Miss Jessie. It straddles the border between Texas and New Mexico Territory, up between the Canadian and Red rivers. But we only stayed there a little while, and of course we didn't register it under our right names. There's quite a bit of stuff hid on it, though, that we've put away from time to time."

"Let's get to it later, then, and go on to your next robbery," Jessie said. "Where was that?"

"Up in Iowa, where we got fifty thousand dollars or so out of the Ocobock Brothers Bank. That was in 'seventy-one. The Younger boys and Clell Miller and Jim White and Jim Koughman was riding with us at the time, so we had to split up our take seven ways. Dingus and I didn't get enough to bury anything, but we wouldn't've had time to, anyhow. The Ocobock people got a posse together and we had to ride hard to get away. They chased us all the way down to the Ozark Mountains in Missouri before we shook them off."

"You and your brother are supposed to have held up a lot of banks in that part of the country, and a few trains, too, if I remember," Jessie said. Her words were more a question than a statement, and Frank James nodded.

"We kept right busy in 'seventy-two and 'seventy-three," he admitted. "We'd put our own bunch together while we were in the Ozarks, and started robbing trains and banks both. Half the holdup men in the country made a beeline for the mountains after a job, so we managed to put by a little bit."

"Did you hide anything in the Ozarks?" Jessie asked.

"Not ever," James said emphatically. "There were too many of our kind hiding out in those hills. As soon as

Dingus and I had enough laid by, we'd take it to our ranch in Texas and put it away where it'd be safe."

"How much do you think you have hidden there right now?" Jessie asked him.

"Well, let me think back a little bit." Frank James frowned thoughtfully. "There was about four thousand dollars from the Saint Genevieve Bank in Missouri, and maybe twenty thousand dollars from the Rock Island train we held up in 'seventy-three outside of Adair, and thirty thousand dollars we got out of the bank in Columbia, down in Kentucky. Then in 'seventy-four we pulled the Gads Hill job in Missouri, there was about seventy thousand dollars from that. And that was the bad luck job, the one that got the railroads to get together and hire the Pinkertons to start after us."

"Is all that hidden on your ranch in Texas?" Jessie probed. "I'd imagine your place in Mexico was too far to get to easily."

"That's just the way it was, Miss Jessie," James said. "Like I said, we had to put in a lot of time hiding out in 'seventy-three and 'seventy-four. One time we had to go clear up to the Green River country in Wyoming to get a little rest."

"I don't see how you managed to get around and cover so much of the country," Jessie told him.

"Well, it wasn't easy," James replied. "We tried to quit once, right after the Pinkertons got after us in 'seventy-four. That was when we were up in Nebraska, in Kearny. We'd made a few friends on the other side of the law by then, and they pulled a string here and there. I don't know whether or not you'd've heard about it down here in Texas, but they managed to get an amnesty bill for Dingus and me into the legislature in Missouri, since that was where we'd been the busiest."

"I remember reading something about it in a newspaper," Jessie replied. "But I wasn't too interested in things like bank holdups and train robberies then."

"Well, the bill didn't pass," James said. "It was a pity, too, because both me and Dingus wanted to get off the owl-hoot trail by then. He'd gotten married, and I was courting."

"How did you manage to find time for courting?" Jessie asked, not even trying to hide her astonishment.

"Robbing a bank or a train doesn't really take a long time, Miss Jessie," James answered. "Maybe a week to plan out a job. And once you start the job it's over in half an hour at the most. You put in another two or three days skedaddling to whatever hideout you're going to use, then you don't have anything to do until you're ready to start figuring out how you'll pull the next job. Oh, there's plenty of time for courting."

"Even with the Pinkertons on your trail?" Ki asked.

"Now, that's a real sore spot for me, Ki," James said. "Allan Pinkerton's not a man that gives up. And he's got some real mean men working for him, like that brother of his. It was old Pinkerton's brother who worked up that scheme to kill Dingus and me with a bomb."

By the time the outlaw had finished speaking, his face was flushed and his body taut and trembling with anger. Jessie, still tired after her experiences of the past two days, saw that it was time to quit stirring Frank James up by having him recall memories of the past.

"I know there's a lot of ground we haven't covered yet," she told him. "But it's getting late and you and Ki must be as tired as I am. Why don't we stop now, and start making this list tomorrow, after we've all had a good night's sleep?"

"Whatever suits you suits me, Miss Jessie," James said.

"But if you don't object, I might sit up awhile and read. And later on, I could work on that list by myself, if it tires you out too much."

"How far are we from being through?" she asked.

"Quite a ways. We only got as far as 'seventy-four, so there's still five years or so to go over," he said. "But if you get tired, I can just sit down by myself, or maybe with Ki, and get it finished up."

"You know that I'll be glad to help you with it, Jessie," Ki volunteered. "There's not much for me to do except keep an eye on the men now and then while they finish gathering the market herd."

"I suppose all three of us could work on it," Jessie said thoughtfully. "I didn't realize what a job it was going to be, or how long it would take."

"I'll tell you what, Miss Jessie," James suggested. "Instead of me reading myself to sleep tonight, I'll just sit here and jot down some notes that'll make it easier to start in the morning."

"If you'll pardon my curiosity, what are you reading?" Jessie asked.

"Oh, nothing I haven't read before," the outlaw said. "I keep going back to old William Shakespeare. He wrote some pretty tough stuff about the old kings, and crooks like Shylock, and a lot of other things that take a man's mind off his own worries."

Hiding her surprise, Jessie said, "If you feel like making a few notes, we can go over them together tomorrow. I can see now that we've got more work to do than I'd realized. And the sooner we finish the preliminaries, the sooner we can start on the real job we've got ahead."

Chapter 9

"This is quite a long list you've given me, Mr. James," Jessie said as she folded the pages together. She and Frank James were sitting in the study. "And—well, I suppose 'impressive' is the best word I can think of to describe the amount of money you and your brother have hidden away. I'm sure you must realize that you're both very rich men."

"We didn't start out to get rich, though," he told her. "We just couldn't find anybody who'd hire on men that had been in Quantrill's Raiders. All we wanted was to get enough money to keep us alive."

"Yes, that might be what a lawyer would call a mitigating circumstance." Jessie nodded. "Of course, I don't approve of outlawry," Jessie went on. "I'd be even more impressed if you'd earned your money honestly instead of breaking the law by taking it at the point of a gun."

"We never did figure folks would call us angels," James replied calmly. "Not even from the time we started with Quantrill, when we were still wet behind the ears."

"I'll be honest with you, Mr. James," Jessie said. "I'd feel a lot better if the object of this job I've taken on was to give the money you've accumulated back direct to the people you stole it from."

"Dingus and I have talked about that more than once," James said. "But we never could figure out a way to do it."

"Would you do it, if Ki and I helped you?"

Ki came into the room just as Jessie mentioned his name. He said, "I'm sorry I interrupted your talk, Jessie. But from what I heard, we're going to start getting busy pretty soon."

"Perhaps even busier that we'd planned," Jessie told him. "I've just suggested to Mr. James that the authorities might be quicker to consider a pardon if he and his brother would return what there is left of their loot to the people they—they stole it from."

"I guess maybe they would, at that." Frank James frowned. "But you'll sure have a lot of tough figuring to do. We didn't bother about who we robbed from, Miss Jessie. Why, half the banks we held up have gone out of business by now, or the folks who owned them years ago have died or sold out to somebody else."

"That's true," Jessie nodded thoughtfully. "The Panic—"

James went on as though she hadn't spoken. "And we never knew whose money or jewelry was in the express-car safes, just like we never knew the names of the folks we cleaned out when we'd go through the passenger coaches."

"I can see where it would really be a problem," Jessie agreed. "But suppose you think about it."

"Why, I'll be glad to," he agreed. "There's only one thing I wouldn't want to happen, though."

"What's that?"

"Not one penny of what we give back goes to the damned—" he stopped abruptly, his face flushing. "Excuse me, Miss Jessie. I've gotten into the habit of talking rough and swearing a lot, and it's a right hard habit to break."

"You don't have to apologize." Jessie smiled. "I've

heard all the words before. But I appreciate your apology. Now, what were you about to tell me?"

"Not one penny of what I hand over to you goes to Allan Pinkerton and his gang. Because that's what he's running, Miss Jessie—a gang. He's got as many crooks and killers working for him as we ever had in the James gang."

"I wouldn't know," Jessie said. "Though after what you told Ki and me last night about that bombing, I can understand how you feel about the Pinkerton agency. But right now, I'm more interested in getting on with the first part of this job I've taken on."

"You're going to go ahead and witness for us, then?" James asked. "And tell the lawmen we surrender to that we're giving back every penny of what we stole?"

"I'm going to keep my word, of course." She nodded. "Later, I'll go over this list you've given me more carefully, but just from glancing at it I'd suggest the logical place to start would be your ranch in Mexico."

"You're thinking of the silver ingots hidden there, I suppose?" Ki asked.

"Yes. If we go to Mexico from the Circle Star, we'll save having to backtrack later," Jessie told him.

"It's the stash we're closest to, all right," James agreed, nodding thoughtfully. "And I guess on the way back you'd want to leave those silver bars here at your ranch, where they'd be safe?"

Jessie shook her head and replied, "I was thinking about something else you mentioned last night. It occurred to me that your ranch in Texas would be the best place to store what we recover. From what you've told us, it's far enough away from the places where you and your brother were the—well, let's say the most active."

"And it'd be closer to a railroad, too, I imagine," Ki put in. "We'd certainly save ourselves a lot of traveling."

"I guess it'd be as good a place as any." The outlaw nodded thoughtfully. "And nobody but me and Dingus even knows that we own that ranch. We didn't use our real names when we bought it, of course. Sure, I'll settle doing that, if it suits you."

"That's fine," Jessie told him. "Now, all we have to do is make a start." She turned to Ki. "Can you get any loose-end chores on the ranch finished up today?"

Ki nodded. "Very easily. We can start tomorrow, if you want to, Jessie."

"We're finally on Rancho Plumada land," Frank James told Jessie and Ki as he reined in and squinted into the westering sun at the high jagged ridge that rose ahead of them. "We'd better rest the horses before we go up that rise. Right past it we'll hit rangeland again. After that, it's just two hours of easy riding to the main house. We'll be there before dark."

"I'll be glad of that," Jessie said as they started toward the ridge. Like Ki, she was riding one of the work-horses from the Circle Star; she valued Sun too greatly to ride him on the risky trip they were undertaking. "It's been quite a ride from the border. I can see now what you meant when you told us you felt safe here."

"It's cut off from everyplace, all right," James agreed. "But in the valley it's got range almost as good as your Circle Star, even if it's not as big. You'll feel right at home."

Jessie nodded. "I'm sure we will."

"One thing I guess I'd better mention before we get there, too," James went on. "Don't be surprised when the foreman calls me by the name I go by here. It's Tom

McKinney, and I guess you and Ki had better call me that, too."

"I'm not even going to ask you right now how many other names you go by," Jessie said. "But we'll remember the one you use here, of course."

They rode on silently in the yellowing light of the declining sun, up the steep slope to its crest. Their mounts were breathing hard again, and by common consent they halted to let the animals rest. Below them, a broad valley opened. Roughly in the center of the valley, along the banks of a thready little creek that widened as it flowed toward the river, a scattered group of perhaps two dozen squat adobe houses straggled around a larger one.

Beyond them there were corrals, then open range again. In the distance, the houses looked little bigger than a child's building blocks. From the cluster of dwellings the rangeland stretched off to the base of still another line of ridges, blue in the distance.

"Those mountains to the west are what the Mexicans call the *Sierra San Martín del Borracho*," James told Jessie and Ki. "If you don't know any of the language, *borracho* means drunk, so I guess even some of the saints got orrey-eyed now and again."

"They were humans before they were saints," Ki said, and smiled. "In the legends of my own country there are some gods and goddesses who had the same human flaws."

Jessie had been sweeping her eyes across the valley. She said, "That range looks very good. And judging by the main house, you've got a fairly large spread here."

"It's big enough," James agreed. "And the graze is a lot better than I ever saw it before, but it's been a while since I was here last. Maybe if you bring off this job you've taken on for me, Miss Starbuck, I'll be able to move here and settle down peacefully."

"You sound as though you'd enjoy doing that," Jessie commented.

James frowned. "I'm not real sure I would. But we can talk about that later on. Right now I'm thinking about that stack of silver ingots that's buried in those foothills."

"How long will it take us to get the silver from where it's hidden?" Ki asked.

"Not more than a day or two," James replied. "The only thing that bothers me is handling it and hauling it. I don't want the hands to know what we're doing, so we'll have to dig out the cave-mouth ourselves and load the silver and haul it to the railroad."

"That won't bother Ki and me one bit," Jessie said. "We'll probably run into other jobs of the same kind later on, so we can start getting used to the idea now."

"Do you have a wagon stout enough to haul that much silver in?" Ki asked. "It's going to be a pretty heavy load."

"It's too heavy a load for us to use a wagon, Ki," James told him. "And there's places where the road's not wide enough for one, anyhow. The only way I can see to get that silver out of here is on pack-critters."

"Pack-mules require handlers," Jessie frowned. "And they might talk too much. Can't the three of us take care of a mule-train by ourselves?"

"I wasn't thinking about mules, Miss Jessie," James said. "This country runs mostly to burros. They're little, but they're not as ornery as mules are, and they're a lot easier to get hold of down here in Mexico."

"I've never tried to manage them," Jessie said. "But I'll do the best I can."

"I've handled mules a little bit, but never burros," Ki put in. "And I feel the same way Jessie does. I'll do my best."

"I'm sure we'll manage," Jessie assured him. "After we've rested a day or two, we'll start back with the silver."

Forging steadily ahead, they'd gotten almost within hailing distance of the houses when a rider emerged from the cluster and came on to meet them.

"That's the foreman," James told Jessie and Ki. "His name is Julio, Julio Flores. A real good man. Dingus and I don't worry a bit about this place because we know he'll be looking after things just as good as we could."

As Flores got within hailing distance, Jessie and Ki examined him. The ranch foreman wore the loose jacket of the country, but his breeches were totally Mexican: tight-legged trousers that flared out below his knees. He was not a young man, as they'd expected him to be. His full mustache was gray, and the long sideburns along his jaws were also grizzled.

"*Bienvenido, patrón!*" he called to Frank James. "I am glad to see you do not forget us."

"Howdy, Julio," James replied. He did not rein in, but kept his horse moving steadily forward. "I guess everything's all right here?"

"*Sí*. We have no trouble. When I see you come close, I am tell Luisa to feex rooms and make beeg *cena*."

"Good." James nodded. "Now, this lady's Miss Jessie, and that fellow's Ki. But we'll only be here a day or two, and we'll be busy out on the range, so don't go getting up a *baile* like you did the last time. But I'll be around to talk to you, and catch up on everything after I've had a chance to wash off the trail dust."

"*Bueno, patrón,*" Julio replied. "*Lo que usted diga, yo hago.*"

They rode on to the ranch house—a rambling, many-roomed adobe structure. The house was much more elaborate than either Jessie or Ki had imagined it would be when Frank James insisted on taking them on an inspection tour.

It was built around a center patio, with the living room and dining room spanning the front, bedroom wings along each side, and the kitchen and servants' quarters along the back.

"You know," James confided to Jessie and Ki as they walked through the patio to the wing containing the rooms which they would occupy, "I can't quite get used to a fancy place like this, but the servants here just went along with the place when I won it, and we didn't try to change anything much. They still do things like I suppose they always did when that rich fellow I won it from had it."

"It's very fine indeed," Jessie said. "I'm surprised that you use it so seldom."

"Oh, Dingus and I talk about moving down here, Miss Jessie," he replied. "But we never could get used to living in such grand style. We just took over the servants and *peones* as part of the deal that was in that poker pot. Besides, even if I do speak the lingo a little bit, Dingus doesn't know it. And our wives would likely feel sorta out of place, too."

He led them to one side of the patio and showed them to bedrooms. "My room's right across the patio," he said. "If the help don't behave to suit you, just knock on my door and let me know."

In her bedroom, Jessie found that in the short time since their arrival, one of the house servants had placed a tray that held a plateful of the small sweet cookies called *biscochos* and a cup of hot chocolate on small tables beside the freshly spread bed. She was tempted to stretch out and doze after the long ride, but was certain that Ki would be tapping on her door soon. He did so even before she'd done more than taste the cup of cinnamon-spiced chocolate.

"Well, what do you think, Jessie?" he asked.

"I'm finally convinced now that Frank James means what he's been saying," she replied. "As far as I can tell from the figures he gave me, the silver bars he says are hidden here make up almost a fourth of the value of the loot he's told us about."

"Do you really think he and his brother will surrender, and give up a place like this?"

"If he wasn't serious, he wouldn't have brought us here," Jessie replied with a thoughtful frown. "He'd have taken us to a cache where there was much less hidden, or simply hauled the silver himself to another hiding-place on the American side of the border."

"Isn't that what we'll be helping him to do?"

"Of course. But nobody's being hurt, Ki. Exactly the opposite, I'd say. It's worth something to everybody in the United States to get the James brothers to surrender. That's all I thought about when I agreed to help him—that, and what he did for you and me."

"As long as you're satisfied, I am, Jessie. You know that."

"Of course I do. And I can't blame you for being suspicious of someone with—"

Jessie broke off when a knock sounded at the door of her room. "Come in," she called.

For a moment both she and Ki stared at the woman who entered in response to Jessie's invitation. The woman was young, her face a shade lighter than the pale bronze of the other people they'd glimpsed at the ranch. Her nose was less aquiline, her chin more softly rounded. Her eyes were what drew the attention of Jessie and Ki, though. They were Mongoloid, and had the tucked inner corner fold that characterized Ki's.

Ki was still staring at the young woman, and she was returning his fixed gaze, when Jessie asked, "What is it that you want?"

"I have come to ask you for supper," she said. Then she quickly corrected herself. "To ask you to come for supper."

Ki paid no attention to her words, but asked, "You're Japanese, aren't you?"

Shaking her head, she replied, "I am not of the full blood. My father came from Japan, but my mother is of this country. And you, *señor?*"

"Just the opposite," Ki told her. "My mother was Japanese, my father was an American. But we do have something in common. We'll find time to talk later."

"Whenever you wish, *señor,* if it does not take me from my work," she said, bowing. "I will tell the *patrón* that I have given you his message."

With another quick bow, she closed the door. Jessie said, "I can't blame you for being surprised, Ki. We'll have to ask Julio about her."

"Yes." He nodded. "Of course, he'd know."

"Or you could ask her instead," Jessie went on. "Perhaps we'll see her again at supper."

Ki shook his head. "It'll wait." He shrugged. "I'm not really all that curious."

When Jessie and Ki left the room they saw that a dinner table had been spread in the patio. Tall silver candelabras stood on the table, dispelling the darkness which had fallen since their arrival. There were also platters holding a roast chicken and a generous roast of beef, bowls of squash and beans, and cloth-wrapped plates containing thin hot tortillas. Frank James was standing beside the table waiting for them.

"Now, one thing we did after we took this place over was to make the women servants stop standing around the table and heaping our plates, whether we wanted anything more or not," he said. "So you just sit down and enjoy

106

your supper."

With all three of them tired after their long trip, they ate scantily and with little conversation. When they'd finished and Jessie sensed from their host's brief remarks between long periods of silence that he would welcome an end to the meal, she pushed her plate away.

"I've had more than enough," she said. "And it's been a long time since daybreak. If you'll excuse me, I'll say good night now. I suppose we can wait until tomorrow to plan our day, can't we, Mr. James?"

"We sure can. And I'm ready for bed myself," he answered quickly, almost eagerly. "So I'll bid you and Ki good night, Miss Jessie, and we'll see if things don't go a lot easier tomorrow than they were on the road here."

Jessie and Ki said good night at the door to her bedroom, and Ki walked down the open corridor to his own room. He opened the door, surprised to find the room in darkness, for he was sure that he'd left a lamp burning. He stepped inside and closed the door, waiting for his eyes to adjust to the darkness of the room when a woman spoke from the midnight gloom.

"Stand where you are while I light the lamp, *Señor* Ki," she said. "I have been waiting for you."

Chapter 10

Ki closed the door and stood waiting beside it. A match flared, and Ki saw the pale oval face of the girl who'd come to summon him and Jessie to supper. He kept his eyes on her as she lifted the glass shade of the lamp that stood on the bedside table and touched the flame to the wick. When she turned back to face him, her face was in shadow and for a moment all that Ki could make out was the outline of her head and shoulders silhouetted against the light.

"Do you really come from my father's country, Ki?" she asked.

"Yes, of course," Ki said. "But you know my name, and I don't know yours."

"I am O-Shi. It was my father's choice. And will you tell me of his country? After I have pleased you, before we go to sleep?"

"You mean you've come to spend the night with me?"

"Of course," the girl answered, as though the question had surprised her. "It would not be courteous to expect a guest of the *estancia* to sleep alone, unless he chooses to do so."

"Whose idea is that?" Ki frowned. "Did Frank James send you here to my room?"

She shook her head. "I have not seen the *hacendado* before today. Such things are arranged by the *mayor-domo*."

While they'd talked, Ki had been covertly examining O-Shi. Her half-Japanese ancestry showed not only in the tucked corners of her eyes, but in the flattened spread of her nose and its bulbous tip, as well as in her high cheekbones and square jawline. She was wearing the same type of clothing which he'd seen on most of the women at the *hacienda:* a full but low-cut *china poblano* blouse with short sleeves and a semicircular neckline that showed the beginning bulges of her small breasts. A full, pleated skirt secured with a loosely-woven cotton waistband fell below her knees. Her bare feet were thrust into flat-heeled *huaraches.*

He asked her, "You mean Julio Flores?"

"Yes. Don Julio always says which one of us is to keep a visitor company. It is a custom of the country."

"And he's picked you out to send to visitors before?"

"Oh, yes. Or to spend a night with him now and then, since he has no wife. Tonight, he selected me to come stay with you because we are both of Japanese blood."

"And you don't mind?"

"Why should I? It is the custom. Besides, most of the men who work here at the *hacienda* are married. There are many of us women and only a few men who have no wives to look after them."

"How long have you been here?" Ki asked.

"Four years. After my father died, my mother came to work at the *estancia.*" As O-Shi talked, a small worried frown began to pucker her face. She asked, "Do I not please you, Ki?"

"Of course you do. You're a very pretty girl, O-Shi."

"Good." Her frown turned into a smile. "Then you will let me stay?"

"Of course," he assured her.

"I will undress you, then. Or do you wish me to take off my clothes first, so that you may caress me while I am removing yours?"

If anything more was needed to emphasize O-Shi's Japanese birthright, Ki read it in her practical, direct approach.

"Why not undress one another?" he suggested.

O-Shi needed no further encouragement. She stepped up close to him and began fingering the sash that he wore at his waist, over his loose blouse. While her hands were busy undoing the waist-cinch and removing his blouse, Ki freed the waistband of O-Shi's full skirt and let the skirt fall to the floor. She raised her arms to pull off Ki's blouse as the skirt slid free. Under her thin petticoat, Ki saw the dark triangle of her bush.

For a few moments after pulling Ki's blouse away, O-shi ran her hands softly over his skin, pressing the corded muscles that rippled in his biceps and forearms. Then she started stroking his sides, her hands moving slowly down to his waist to push the waistband of his loosely-fitting trousers down his hips. The trousers fell to the floor in a huddle and for a moment O-Shi was baffled by the crisscross folds of his cache-sex, the cotton sash that he wore wrapped twice around his waist. Its loose end was brought up under his crotch and tucked into the bands that encircled his hips.

While O-Shi's hands were busy, Ki had slipped the low-cut neck of her *china poblana* blouse over O-Shi's shoulders. She shrugged and twisted her arms, giving up her attentions to his cache-sex until the blouse slid down to join her skirt. Then her fingers returned to the sash. At last she found the proper folds to pull and the long strip of cotton cloth dropped, freeing Ki's swollen erection.

"Oh!" she gasped. "You're much bigger than I'd thought you'd be! You'll have to come into me very slowly, Ki."

"Then suppose you be the one to decide how slowly you want to take me," Ki suggested. He lay down on the bed and stretched out on his back.

Looking down at him, O-Shi said slowly, "That is something I have seen pictured in the *ukiyo-e* I found in my father's sea-chest," she said. "But I have never done what they show."

Ki nodded. "If you've looked at *ukiyo-e* you'll know what I mean," he told her. "Do as you've seen in them."

O-Shi joined him, holding herself above his jutting shaft while she straddled his hips. Then she placed him and started to lower her hips, slowly at first, then faster. Small sighs began pouring from her lips while she sank lower and lower, her eyes growing wider as their bodies came closer together. Then with a final happy cry she let herself go and dropped her body, and Ki's upthrust shaft impaled her fully.

For a few moments O-Shi did not move. Then she began to rock back and forth in a slow, measured rhythm. As the minutes ticked by her swaying hips moved faster and still faster. Her hands were pressing on Ki's shoulders now, her hips gyrating and twisting. Ki brought up his head. His lips found the dark rosettes of her small, firm breasts, and as O-Shi continued her increasingly frantic bucking he caressed their budded tips with his lips and tongue.

Suddenly O-Shi's body began to tremble. Her shudders grew in intensity, her sobbing gasps shook her violently. Ki

111

grasped her hips when a joyous cry escaped her throat, and he helped to guide her wild gyrations until the tremors shaking O-Shi told him that she was nearing a climax.

He waited until he felt the first spastic shudders begin to jerk her squirming body, then grasped her hips firmly and pulled her to him. He held her firmly until O-Shi's final sigh of completion escaped her lips, then he pulled her down and clasped his arms around her while her tremblings faded and passed and at last she lay quietly content.

After a few moments O-Shi raised her head and looked down at him. "You have seen more than I did in the *ukiyo-e*," she said softly. "I did not really understand them until now. But there are many pictures, Ki. Do you know them all?"

"Nobody can see all of them," Ki told her. "There must be thousands of *ukiyo-e*. But I've seen enough to give us ideas we can enjoy for the rest of the night."

"Not just the rest of this night," O-Shi sighed. "But all the nights while you stay here. Now, shall we start again?"

"I can tell from here that nobody's been near our stash," Frank James told Jessie and Ki as they rode along the bank of the little creek that wound like a loose thread across the high-grassed rangeland south of the *hacienda*. He pointed ahead, to a spot where the grass thinnned and the rough contours of a stretch of chalky white stone broke the level surface.

"It's just a limestone outcrop," Jessie said, frowning. "I don't see anything unusual about it."

"Maybe you haven't been around limestone a lot, Miss Jessie," James said. "But when Dingus and me were growing up back in Missouri, there were limestone outcrops all around the farm. We found out real fast that a lot of them had caves in them, so when we came across that little limestone hummock ahead the first thing we thought about was a cave."

"And you found one?" Ki asked.

"Sure as shooting we did!" James replied. "One day right after we'd bought this ranch. We had all those silver ingots, and what was left from our winnings in that big poker game, and needed a safe place to hide 'em. The minute we saw limestone we thought about a cave, and sure enough, there it was."

"I certainly don't see any sign of it," Jessie said as they reined in beside the chalky rock.

"You're not supposed to, Miss Jessie," James said, and smiled. "And neither is anybody else but me or Dingus. Now, I can tell in a minute that nobody has noticed it, either. It's just like we left it."

He swung off his horse and walked over to the outcrop. After studying it for a moment he walked out onto its humped surface and began pulling at a big boulder. After watching him for a moment, Ki dismounted and went to help him. The jagged humps that broke the surface of the big boulder gave them handholds, and under their combined efforts the boulder shifted an inch in the dirt into which it was embedded, then gave way and rolled aside to reveal an opening big enough for a man to crawl into.

James lowered himself into the gaping hole and disappeared. After a moment his head and shoulders emerged. His usually impassive face bore a wide grin. "Everything's just the way we left it," he told Jessie and Ki. "If you'd like to take a look, come on over."

Jessie swung off her horse and picked her way across the broken surface. While she was approaching, James levered himself out of the cave's opening. When Jessie reached his side, he extended his hand.

"Just steady yourself and step down," he told her.

"You'll have to sorta jump down, because you're a lot shorter than me, but I'll hang onto your hand till your feet hit bottom."

Once her feet touched the stone, Jessie found it was easy to hunker down and look into the semidarkness of the domed cavern that opened beyond the entrance. After her eyes had grown accustomed to the deeply shaded interior, she could make out the tiers of silver ingots that rose above its floor as well as a dozen or more bundles wrapped in canvas. Though she knew the value of the loot at which she was gazing, its appearance was so prosaic as to be unexciting. She studied it for a few moments longer, then stood up.

"Well?" Frank James asked. "It's just like I told you it'd be, safe as the day we put it here."

She nodded. "It certainly is." She extended her hand and Ki grasped it to help her out of the cave opening. Turning to Frank James, she went on: "That opening's so small that it's going to take a long time to get all those ingots out."

"Now, don't worry about that, Miss Jessie," he told her. "Next time, I'll bring along a sledgehammer from the ranch house. Limestone breaks real easy, it'll only take about six whacks to open that hole up good."

"Then two or three days ought to see us finished with it," Jessie said.

"Just about," James agreed. "Then it'll take another day to load up a string of burros to haul it to the railroad line. It's only about a day from here."

"Are there enough burros on the ranch?" Jessie frowned.

"Maybe not, but I'd bet Julio can round up however many more we'll need from the other ranches close by."

"And the next stop will be your place in Texas?" Ki asked.

"It would be, the way Miss Jessie figured things out," James said. "But I haven't had time to talk to her about a new idea that popped into my head."

"This is as good a time as any," Jessie said. "Suppose you tell me now."

"Why, sure." He nodded. "Now, there's one more place that we could stop at before we go to that Texas stud farm, Miss Jessie. It's not very far from there, at least."

"Exactly where is it?" Jessie asked.

"Just on the east edge of Colorado, a little ways inside the state line. If you don't know the country around there, it's about in the middle of the fork where the Two Butte River flows into the Arkansas. We picked it out because there's no Wanteds out in Colorado for either Dingus or me," James explained. "And it's not too far from that place we've got down in Texas."

"You don't have any other hiding-places between here and your Texas ranch, if I remember," Jessie said, frowning. "And going to your place in Texas by way of Colorado would save backtracking. I suppose that's what we'd better plan to do."

"I sort of figured you might see it that way," James nodded. "And once we get to the stud ranch, we can stop again and rest up. There's not any Wanteds out on me in Texas or New Mexico, either. All we'd have to worry about is the Pinkertons."

"I've heard they never give up," Ki said.

"You sure heard right, Ki," James agreed. "That's why Dingus and me are being so careful these days. It's one reason that decided us to split up a few months ago. We figured that as long as we were traveling together it wouldn't take much more than a good long look for some-body to place us."

"Now that we've decided what we're going to do next, we'd better get busy," Jessie suggested. "The sooner we start back, the better."

"Another good long day after this one will get us to the railroad," Frank James told Jessie.

They'd stopped to rest the burros and horses on the crest of a long uphill stretch where the trail had zigzagged back and forth for several miles. Ahead, past a thicket of the chaparral that grew thickly on both flanks of the ridge, they saw that the path they'd be following was still one sharp curve after another. But beyond the long downslope the ground leveled out and the beaten track ran straight to the horizon. Overhead the declining sun hung in an almost colorless sky.

"I'll admit that I won't mind changing this saddle for a seat in a coach," Jessie said. "Particularly since we still have a few more long rides ahead of us."

Ki came up to join them. He'd dismounted when they stopped and walked along the line of burros, checking the cinches of the packsaddles that held the dozens of bags into which they'd put the silver ingots for transportation.

"Everything's in good shape," he announced. "As soon as the animals have had enough of a breather, we can get started again."

"They've rested long enough," James said. "And it'll be a lot easier on them, going down that long downstretch ahead. We might as well move on, if you're ready, Miss Jessie."

"As ready as I'll ever be," Jessie replied.

She swung into her saddle, and the men followed suit. They spaced themselves out along the string of burros,

116

Frank James in the lead, Jessie near the center of the pack-animals, and Ki at the rear end of the line. They moved on down the slope and into the high *chamisal* that grew densely on each side of the trail. The greenish-brown leaves of the brush were shoulder-high, so that the riders could see only the heads of their companions as they moved along the winding path.

Jessie's first warning that they'd run into trouble was the booming report of Frank James's revolver. It was followed by the sharper crack of a rifle, and a medley of shouts in Spanish from the growth on both sides of the trail. Then James's voice rose over the scattered reports.

"Holdup, Miss Jessie!" he called. "Look out for bandits in the brush!"

Jessie had drawn her Colt when the sound of the first shot broke the quiet air. She looked around on both sides of the trail, but the *chamisal* was so thick that she could see nothing. She slid out of her saddle and crouched behind her horse just as Ki called a warning from the end of the burro-train.

"Outlaws, Jessie!" he shouted. "They're in the brush on both sides of us!"

Jessie did not reply. She was too busy trying to peer into the dense undergrowth that hemmed them in on both sides of the narrow trail. A shot rang out from the thicket, then another, and she saw the brush shaking a few yards distant. She triggered off a shot into the spot where she'd seen the disturbed *chamisal,* but it had no result that she could make out, and she was too experienced in ambushes to waste scarce bullets on empty space.

There was another burst of shooting from the head of the pack-train—high-pitched reports from rifles, followed by the duller sound of James's pistol. Bullets were singing through the air behind her as well, but in spite of her efforts to find a target in the *chamisal* on either side, she could see nothing.

Suddenly a fresh medley of yells broke the silence and more shooting broke out in the thickets on both sides of the trail. A man's voice sounded in the middle distance:

"Ándense, hombres! Disparen! Que no nos evaden los bandidos!" he called, his voice both loud and hoarse.

Other cries followed on the heels of the shouted command, and the rustlings in the brushes grew louder. Then hoofbeats in broken rhythms thudded in the suddenly silent air, followed by a few scattered shots in the distance.

Overriding the fading sounds of the now-distant hoofbeats and the report of an occasional shot, the loud, hoarse voice of the man who'd called out before rose in the suddenly still air.

"Somos Rurales!" he shouted. *"Yo soy el comandante! Mis hombres han derrotado los bandidos! No tiren más!"*

When she heard the shout identifying the man who'd spoken, Jessie began pushing her way toward the head of the line of silver-laden burros. Frank James was standing beside his horse. He still held his revolver in his hand.

"You heard what that man just said?" Jessie asked him.

"Why, sure, Miss Jessie. And I was real glad to hear him, too. If I know the Rurales, they'll make short work out of those rascals who jumped us."

"But what about you?" She frowned.

"I don't have a thing to worry about," James assured her. "The Rurales aren't after me; I've got a clean slate down here in Mexico. Just don't forget my name, though. As far as the Rurales are concerned, I'm Tom McKinney, and we're just taking these burros to the railroad to load our personal belongings on the train to send to my ranch in Texas."

Chapter 11

Just as Frank James stopped speaking, a man on horseback pushed through the brush at the side of the trail. His eyes grew wide when he saw Jessie and her companion.

"*Son norteamericanos!*" he gasped, then shook his head. He said, "*Señor, señorita.*" Then, switching to almost unaccented English, he went on, "I am Diego Urrutia, *capitán* of the Rurales. Were any of your companions wounded by their shots?"

"We're just fine, Captain," James replied quickly. "I'm Tom McKinney, and this young lady is Miss Jessie Starbuck. We've only got one more man with us, and he's around close somewhere. Likely you know about my place over to the west of here, the Rancho Plumada."

"But of course! It is part of the territory my men patrol," the Rurale said, nodding. He gestured toward the burros. "I hope the bandits did not rob you of anything?"

"They wouldn't've gotten much except some personal truck I'm taking back to the States with me," James replied. "It's lucky you and your men were close enough to us to get here in time."

"We have been on their trail for weeks," the Rurale

said. "When we heard the shooting we were only a short distance away, so naturally we hurried to investigate."

Jessie was watching the two men, her surprise growing greater by the minute. Frank James' manner was as casual as it had always been; if he felt any nervousness he showed no signs of it. She decided at once that unless one of the two men addressed her directly, she'd stay out of their conversation.

"We're just going as far as the railroad line, to Morelos," James went on. "And I don't expect there'll be another bunch of bandits give us trouble."

"Of that, I can assure you, *Señor* McKinney," Urrutia said. "And speaking of the bandits, I must go and see what my men are doing. You will understand, I'm sure."

"Of course we do," James replied. "Thanks for your help, Captain. I hope I'll see you the next time I come back to the ranch."

With a bow to Jessie and a salute to Frank James, the Rurale swung into his saddle and pushed into the brush. James waited until the sounds of his progress had faded away, then turned to Jessie.

"Well, I don't see much reason for—" he began. Then there was a rustle in the brush. Ki pushed through the dense undergrowth and joined them beside the trail.

"I stopped when I heard who you were talking to," he told James. "I didn't want to give you anything else to explain to that Rurale, and perhaps get him started asking questions."

"There wasn't much danger of that," James replied. "You see, Ki, it's just like I told Miss Jessie. As far as the law in Mexico is concerned, I'm just a rich Yankee fool who owns a ranch down here."

"I was surprised when he didn't ask any more questions," Jessie said. "But what you told him must've satisfied him. He just went on about his business as though finding us here with a big pack-train was the most normal thing in the world."

"Sure." James smiled. "And it is, down here south of the border. He didn't have any reason to suspect I'm an outlaw on the other side of the Rio Grande, and if I'm lucky, I'll keep these folks from finding out for a long time. Now, if we're going to get to the railroad line in time to catch that train, we'd better be pushing along."

"Are you sure that you don't want me to handle the reins for a little while?" Jessie asked Frank James as the heavily laden wagon lurched over the bumpy trace of a road that stretched across the prairie ahead. She'd just settled back on the wagon-seat after turning and leaning around the canvas cover to make sure that Ki was still following them in the second wagon.

"No thanks, Miss Jessie," Frank James replied. "We'll be getting to the stud farm, such as it is, in about two more hours, and I'm not all that tired."

"It's been a long trip, though," she went on. "I'll be glad to have the few days of rest we're planning on."

"Well, now, when you come right down to it, so will I," he told her. "Because we've still got a lot of traveling to do before we're finished."

She nodded. "Yes, I know. But if I remember correctly, we can go by train to the rest of the places where your loot's hidden."

"That's right," he said, nodding. "The furthest one away is up in the Powder River country, and there are two more south of the river in Wyoming Territory. We'll have a comfortable place to stay up there, though. Nigger John's got a real nice house and a good bunkhouse on his horse farm. If you come down to it, we'll be a mite more comfortable there than we will at the place we're heading for now. It's not such a much for looks, but it'll be a safe place to shelter."

"You've got so many places that I can't keep track of them," Jessie said, and smiled. "But I suppose the old saying's true about there being safety in numbers."

"Well, ever since we got on the owl-hoot trail, Dingus and I have needed a lot of safe places to get into. And they're not just for the two of us. We use them to shelter the boys that ride with us if they get shot up or hurt. Like the one we're heading for now. Poor old Joab Perry never did get real well after he was hurt so bad in that mess we made up in Northfield, so we put him in charge of the place."

"But that's been four or five years ago!" she exclaimed.

"Oh, you don't have to remind me when it was, Miss Jessie. I don't guess I'll ever get over being mad at myself for making all the mistakes I did when I led the boys in there."

Though James's remarks had stirred Jessie's curiosity, she hesitated for a moment before saying, "I've read so many different versions of what happened there that I'm still confused about it. Everyone seems to think you and your brother were the leaders of the group, but I haven't been sure until now that you were really involved."

"Oh, it was Dingus and me and our regular boys, all right," James told her.

Jessie could read a strain of anger in his voice, as well as a tinge of sorrow or regret. She'd grown used to Frank James' usual emotionless way, and the reaction he'd shown when she mentioned the Northfield bank robbery surprised her.

"Please," she said, "don't talk about it if it's going to upset you."

122

"It takes a lot of upsetting to stir me up any more, Miss Jessie." James smiled. "It's even stopped bothering me when Dingus and I get blamed for a lot of jobs that we never were anywhere near. I deserve more of the blame for that Northfield mixup than Dingus does. I don't mind telling you, I'd put away a lot more whiskey than was good for me, that day."

"I've never seen you take more than a swallow or two." She frowned.

"I don't, anymore. Northfield cured me of drinking, or came pretty close to it. But if you want the real unvarnished truth of what happened, I don't mind telling you, as long as you don't talk about it to anybody else."

"Of course I won't," she promised. "And please don't tell me, if talking about it bothers you."

"Talking about it to somebody like you might do me good," James said. "I guess you have heard a lot of yarns that don't make sense. If you're of a mind to listen, I'll tell you what really happened."

"I certainly won't say no," Jessie replied. "Go ahead, then."

"Well, the first thing is that we didn't start out for that Northfield bank," James began. "Dingus and me had taken a look at it a day or so before, while we were waiting for the boys we'd picked out for the job to get there. We hadn't worked up a real scheme to handle the Northfield job, though. We'd figured the Mankato bank out first, so that's where we went when we got up that day."

Frank James paused and Jessie could see that he was looking back into the past. When he showed no signs of continuing, she reminded him of her presence.

"How far is it from Mankato to Northfield?"

"Oh, I made it out to be thirty miles, give or take a few steps. We'd holed up just south of Mankato to wait while our boys got there. Clell Miller and Charlie Pitts and Bill Chadwell got there first, but the Younger brothers got mixed up on the place we'd picked to meet, so they got in late."

"How many Younger brothers were there then?" Jessie asked. "Didn't one of them get killed?"

"Not at Northfield, Miss Jessie. That was later. Cole and Jim and Bob were all with us at Mankato, but nothing happened there. They all three got hurt in Northfield, but it was more like being scratched up than anything else. Shucks, there wasn't one of us that didn't get hurt there."

"Including you?"

"Oh, sure. I took a rifle slug in my leg and Dingus lost a little bit of skin. But we got out alive, and so did the Younger boys. But I got off the track of telling you how it all came about." James frowned.

"Yes. You haven't told me yet why you didn't go ahead with your original plan in Mankato."

"That was our big mistake, but it made sense to pass up the job after we'd looked at the Mankato bank. We got a late start from where we'd camped, and when we got to town there were men stirring around on the street, and a crew of carpenters working at putting a new room on the bank. I told the boys to wait while I went in for a look-see, and after I got inside I didn't much like what I saw."

"There were too many people around?" Jessie prodded when James fell silent again.

"Too many that had on pistol-belts," James said nodding. "I saw in a minute why they were there. The whole side of the building where the vault stood was wide open, so I figured the bank had hired guards to keep anybody from just helping themselves."

"That's why you called off the robbery, then?"

James nodded. "That was the main reason. We rode out

of town a ways and talked things over. We had a few drinks while we were palavering, and finally we decided to go back for another look. Things hadn't changed any, so we rode back to where we'd been camped and talked some more."

"That must've been when you decided to go to Northfield, then," Jessie guessed when he fell silent again.

He nodded. "About the middle of the night. All of us had put away a little bit too much liquor by then, and the Younger boys didn't like giving up because they'd had a long ride to get there and didn't want to go back home without something to show for their trip. So about three o'clock in the morning we started riding to Northfield."

"You mean you didn't sleep at all the night before you held up the bank there?"

"It was a two-day ride to get there, Miss Jessie, and we didn't sleep much either night. We didn't carry much grub, but we had more whiskey than we needed. Let's see, I told you that Dingus and I had made about half a plan after we looked at the town while we were waiting for the Younger boys. Well, we put the fine points on that plan during those two nights it took us to get there. We stopped just outside town the second night and put the fine points on our scheme. Next morning we rode the rest of the way into town and had breakfast at the only restaurant there was there. And right after breakfast we scattered, and the trouble started."

With her keen perception, Jessie had noticed that James had been bringing extraneous details into his story since the first mention of Northfield. She decided to prod him gently, to get him back on the main thread of his story again.

"According to most of the stories I remember hearing and reading, you didn't even get into the bank," she said.

125

"That's right," the outlaw said, nodding. "But Dingus told me all about what happened, and I saw the rest myself. What our plan was, Jim Younger and Bill Chadwell and me were supposed to keep the townsfolk off the street so we could make a clean getaway. Cole Younger and Clell Miller were the outside guards, and Dingus led Bob Younger and Charlie Pitts inside to clean out the safe and the money-tills. But our plan didn't work out like most others we'd made."

"Why?" Jessie asked when James paused again. "Didn't your men do what they were supposed to?"

"Oh, none of them fell down on their jobs," James replied. "But a lot of things happened that we hadn't counted on. Dingus and Bob and Charlie had trouble inside. The safe was locked and none of the bank folks would open it, so they started gathering up what they could from the tellers, and that took time. Then, when Clell tried to stop a fellow from going in and seeing Jesse and Bob and Charlie, the fellow tumbled to what we were doing and started yelling. And about three minutes after that, the lead began flying."

"Who shot first?" Jessie asked. "You'd remember that, I'm sure."

"Oh, I remember all right," James replied. "It was Clell Miller. He tried to cut down the fellow he'd stopped from going inside the bank. The way it turned out, that fellow had a hardware store right next door to the bank. When Clell kept him from going inside, the fellow ran back inside his store and picked up his rifle and started shooting at Clell and Cole. He dropped Clell with his first shot, then he yelled for anybody who wanted a gun to come get one. That's what really beat us."

"But even if that man in the store was handing out guns,

it would've taken time for him to pass out very many," Jessie said. "That should have given you time to get away. You just said a minute ago that you and two of your other men were to keep people off the streets."

"So I did," James agreed. "And that's what we started doing when we heard the first shooting. The three of us spread lead all over the place. The thing about it was that we were outside shooting and the men that had gone in the hardware store holed up in it and were pot-shooting at us. And about then, Charlie Pitts shot at one of the bank tellers and missed, and he ran out and started yelling before Charlie could follow him outside. And about then somebody began sniping at Bill and Jim and me from a store down the street."

As James talked, his words had come tumbling out faster and faster, in contrast to his usual deliberate manner of speech. He stopped now to catch his breath.

Not wanting to risk him ending his story without finishing it, Jessie said quickly, "But unless I'm wrong, all of you men rode with Quantrill during the war. You must've been used to facing gunfire."

"It's different during a war, Miss Jessie," he replied soberly. "Sure, we got shot at and we shot back, but everybody expected that to happen. Our bunch hadn't been shot at much since the war ended, and there was Clell Miller already down, and I had a piece of lead in my leg before Dingus and Cole and Bill got out of the bank. Charlie Pitts came out first, and somebody cut him down before he could get to his horse. Then Dingus and Cole popped out of the door and both of them got hit, but not bad enough to keep them from mounting up. So the upshot was that eight of us rode into that damn town—" James stopped and shook his head. "Sorry, Miss Jessie, I don't swear much,

127

but I guess I got sort of excited. Anyhow, there were only five of us when we turned tail and ran. And I still feel ashamed now when I say that."

"I've heard all the words before," Jessie told him calmly. "What were you about to say?"

"Oh, sure." James nodded. "There were eight of us when we rode in and five when we rode out. And I don't suppose I could say this to anybody else, but you've got a way of understanding what a man tells you. I could see that the first time we talked, after I'd helped you and Ki run off those Mexicans who'd gotten you holed up. I guess I've talked more to you about that mess we made in Northfield than I have to anybody else except Dingus. And we don't talk about it anymore, but I'll have to say, it's eased my mind a lot, digging out what happened and telling you about it."

"I'll keep the promise I made you," Jessie said. "I won't say a word about what you've told me to anybody—unless you wouldn't mind me telling Ki."

"I set a good deal of store in both of you," James told her. "But I guess you'd've noticed that."

"Perhaps that's because we're doing what we can to help you," she suggested.

Frank James shook his head. "No. I appreciate your help, all right. But I wouldn't've asked you until after we'd had our first real talk."

"And I wouldn't've said yes and changed my mind twice if you hadn't proved you'd changed by helping me when you didn't have to," Jessie told him. "Now, I feel just about the way you do. We'll both forget what we've been talking about."

"That's the best thing to do," James agreed. "And we're only about four miles from the stud farm now. We can stay there a few days while we clean up the hidey-holes close by, and then I guess we'll have to head for Wyoming, and what we get there and on the way up to the Powder River country and back will just about finish up the job."

Chapter 12

"By gum, Frank, you're a real sight for sore eyes!" the gangly man called as he limped up to the wagon in which Frank James and Jessie were riding. "And I see you brought somebody to keep you company."

"This lady is Miss Jessica Starbuck, Joab," Frank James told the man, stressing the "Miss." "And she's a real lady, not the kind that you and me and the rest of our bunch are used to being around. Now, see that you remember that."

"Oh, sure." Joab nodded. He turned to Jessie and went on: "I hope you won't look too close at the way things are here, Miss Starbuck. But I guess you seen I ain't in as good shape as I'd like to be. This game leg of mine don't seem to want to mend up the way it oughta, but I'm doing the best I can."

"I'm accustomed to making do when I have to," Jessie said. "And we're not going to be here very long. We just need a few days to rest up; then we'll start traveling again."

Ki's wagon rolled up and came to a stop beside the one in which Frank James and Jessie were still sitting.

"I suppose this is where we stop?" he asked James.

"It sure is, Ki," James replied. He gestured to the sprawl of unpainted, weatherbeaten buildings that stood in front of them. "I know it doesn't look much like you expected it to, after seeing that ranch in Mexico, but Dingus and I just bought this little spread a few years ago, and haven't had time to fix it up very much."

Joab broke in. "Frank, I haven't had time to finish telling you what was in my mind when I seen you roll up. Jesse was here till just three days ago. It's too bad you didn't get here before he had to go. He said to tell you—"

"You can tell me what the two of you talked about later on, Joab," James broke in quickly. "Right now, you'd better take care of getting things in the house fixed up as best you can so that we'll all have a place to sleep tonight."

"Sure." Joab nodded, looking at the wooden crates that were stacked in the wagon-beds. "I guess you'll want me to give you a hand unloading that stuff, too."

"Later, maybe. Not now," James said quickly. "Everything except our saddlebags can just stay in the wagons for now. We'll finish unloading later on."

"Whatever you say," Joab replied. "Now, I better hyper over to the house and do a mite of sweeping up before you settle in. I've been feeling so poorly lately, I ain't done the housekeeping chores real regular-like."

As Joab limped away, Frank James turned to Jessie and Ki and said, "I don't suppose Joab realizes that he's never going to be able to ride much again. But he'll be all right here, and he's about the only one who was handy when Dingus and I bought this place. Now let's just pull the wagons up closer to the house and unhitch the horses. We'll decide later where to put these boxes."

"You don't have a regular hiding place here, then?" Jessie asked as Frank James slapped the reins over the back of the horse and the wagon rolled slowly up to the sprawled-out frame house.

"Not yet, Miss Jessie," Frank said. "We haven't had this

131

place long enough to poke around it much. But there's a big rock formation just a little ways east, close to the Texas line, that might have a cave or a ravine that'd make a good stash. We can go look at it after we've rested up awhile."

"This looks like very good range," Jessie commented. She stood up on the wagon-seat as James reined in the horse and they came to a stop. Gazing from one horizon to the other, she asked the cattle rancher's perennial question: "Is there enough water on it to support a cattle herd of any size?"

James nodded. "More'n likely there is. But it makes more sense for Dingus and me to make it a horse ranch. The fellow that sold us the place says you only have to dig down about twenty feet to hit underground water. We'd need to put up a windmill wherever we want to pull it up, of course."

"Or dig stock-ponds like I have on the Circle Star," Jessie said. "I don't suppose there are any creeks around?"

"No, but there's the Canadian River, about a mile to the north, except that I've been told it's dry most of the summer in this part of Texas."

Ki had finished maneuvering the wagon he was handling into a position behind the first one. He came up in time to hear Frank James' reply. He asked, "We're in Texas, then?"

"We are right now," James assured him. "Our property line runs in a sort of vee, pointing east. The point of the vee is only about fifteen miles away from Tascosa. That's where Dingus and I met the fellow we bought this place from. It's the nearest town to us. And while I'm thinking about it, my name here is Al McKinney, if we go into town."

"I'd just as soon stay away from towns," Jessie said. "As soon as you've found a safe place and we get those boxes in the wagons hidden away, let's start for the Powder River country."

"Whatever you say, Miss Jessie," Frank James agreed. "I know this trip's been real tiring, but we'll all feel better after we've rested a few days. Then we'll get on with gathering up what's in the rest of the stashes and see if Dingus and I have any luck swapping our loot for some kind of pardon."

Jessie shielded her eyes with the palm of her hand and gazed ahead at the hillocky, grass-tufted prairie they were now crossing in the southwestern corner of Wyoming Territory. Even with their own livery-rented mounts and the two packhorses led by Ki and Frank James, they made a small, lonely-looking group as they rode across the seemingly endless expanse of short-grass, the declining sun in their faces.

Turning to James, Jessie remarked, "You and your brother certainly hid your loot in a lot of different places, Mr. James."

"We had some pretty good reasons for doing it, Miss Jessie," James told her. "But Dingus wasn't with me when I hid this batch. But you're right about us having a lot of stuff put away in different places. You've got to remember how it is with outlaws like we are."

"I'm afraid I've never been an outlaw," Jessie reminded him. "So I wouldn't know how it is."

"Well now, when you've pulled off a job and the law gets on your trail, you can't afford to stop just anyplace and everyplace," he went on. "You ride fast and put as many miles as you can between you and whoever's after you. Of course, when it's lawmen chasing you, the easiest way to shake them off is to run to where they don't have any jurisdiction."

"That would make sense," Ki commented. "But it certainly wouldn't make them feel any kinder toward you."

"They wouldn't feel kind anyways, Ki." James smiled. Then he added, "Of course, we had another reason to run a long way from where we'd pull a job. State and county lines don't stop the Pinkertons like they do sheriffs and marshals, you know. When the Pinkertons started chasing us, right after we robbed that train at Gads Hill, we had to move faster and run further than we ever had before."

"So that's when you started spreading out your hiding places?" Jessie asked him.

"Oh, we'd been doing that a long time, Miss Jessie," he replied. "After we pulled off a job we'd always hide our takings as soon as we could find a good place. That way, if we got caught they wouldn't find any evidence against us. What we're going to dig up now is from a train we held up just outside of Medicine Bow."

"Why, that's one of the towns we passed through on the train we took to Rock Springs!" Jessie exclaimed.

"Sure," James nodded. "Back in 'seventy-seven, when Dingus wanted to stay back in Missouri with Zelda and wait for their baby to get born, we split up. I rode with Big Nose Parrot and his boys for a while; then Ol Sheppard and Bid McDaniels and me cut loose from Big Nose's outfit. We held up two or three trains, and it wasn't long before there were posses looking for us all over the place. We split up, and I headed for Brown's Hole to hide out, but I tucked away my share of the take before I got there."

"I hope this loot we're going after now isn't as hard to get to as some of the places in the Indian Nation," Ki put in. "And I hope that there aren't as many mosquitoes guarding it."

"We won't have any trouble, Ki," James promised.

"And we won't have to do any swimming, or wading in bog-mud like we had to do back there."

"How long will it take us to get to the horse farm after we clear out the places where the money is?" Jessie asked.

"About four days. If we push on the rest of the day like we've been doing, we'll get to the gorge before it's too dark to see. It won't take more than an hour or two for me to get to where my stash is. Then we can turn around tomorrow and start for the horse farm. We won't have to worry about the Pinkertons then, because Nigger John can smell a lawman a mile off."

They pushed on as the sun dropped lower and lower until it dipped below the peaks of the Wasatch Mountains, a hundred miles away. Even after the last sliver of its rim disappeared, it continued to light the sky. The land had been growing progressively rougher since a short time before sunset, grass giving way in huge areas to outcrops of barren stone. It rose ahead of them in a perceptibly upward slant as well, and as they drew closer to the river gorge the tired horses moved more and more slowly.

"We'd better start looking for a place to stop before it gets too dark," Frank James said. "Pretty soon we'll hit the rocks and there won't be any graze for our animals."

Jessie pointed to a clump of low-growing cedars about a quarter of a mile ahead and said, "That's about the best-looking place I can see. Those cedars might mean there's water close by it. Shall we head for it?"

"Why, that's the place I've been looking for these past two or three miles, Miss Jessie," James said. "And there's water there, all right. I knew it was someplace close to the trail, but I couldn't recall how far along it was. That's where I nighted over when I passed this way before."

"You lead the way, then," Ki suggested. "I'm as ready as anybody to call it a day."

135

A thin covering of earth, and dry vegetation that had been shed by the cedars, covered the hard rock around the spot Jessie had noticed. Near the center of the clumped dwarf cedars the tiny trickle of a spring made a pool two or three hand-spans wide and only a few inches deep. Old, long-dry horse-droppings, mingling with the small ribbed dung of antelopes and the faint wind-eroded impressions of shod hooves around the perimeter of the cedar stand, showed that other travelers as well as the animals native to the region had used the spring before them.

"We might as well camp here. I'll scramble down to that ledge where my stashes are tomorrow morning," Frank James suggested as they munched a spartan supper of cheese and jerky and hardtack. "It's an easy walk to the rim, and the ledge they're on's not more than forty or fifty feet down the side of the gorge. If I put two of our lariats together they'll give me a long enough rope. And the stuff is stowed in cracks in the rock-face. I just filled them in with loose stones. I had to hurry when I was putting it away because that morning I'd spotted a posse chasing after me. I shook 'em off about noon, but I was worried that they might catch up with me again."

"What you hid here's not bulky, then?" Jessie asked.

"No, but it's heavy," James replied. "Bags of gold coins and some jewelry from a train Dingus and me and the Younger boys held up. It was a real good haul; there were two safes stuffed with bank shipments and about a bucketful of jewelry we got from the passenger cars."

"It it's too heavy for you to climb back up with alone, I'll be glad to go with you and help you," Ki offered.

"That'd sure make it a lot easier, Ki, if you've got a notion to lend me a hand." James said. "And if Miss Jessie won't mind staying by herself for a while . . ."

"Being by myself won't bother me a bit," Jessie said. "I'll just stay here and take life easy, unless you need me to help, too."

"Oh, Ki and I can handle it all right," James told her. "I didn't have help putting it down where it is. All I did was drop the bags one at a time to a ledge that's about twenty feet down from the rim. Then I left my rope dangling so I could climb out. But getting those bags down there's one thing. Hauling them up is going to be more of a job."

"Will you have it up in time for us to start back tomorrow?" Jessie asked.

James shook his head. "Not likely, Miss Jessie. It'll take me and Ki most of the day. I figure it's about a two-hour ride to the place on the rim of the gorge where that shelf widens out. Then after we get to it, we'll have to shinny down a rope to the ledge. It'll take me a while to uncover the crannies where I stored the stuff. After that, we'll have the bags to hoist up and carry back. But we can start for the horse farm at daybreak the next day, if that suits you."

"Oh, I'm not trying to hurry you," Jessie said. "I'll just rest and not do much of anything while you're gone. I might even take my rifle and see if I can bring down an antelope. Some fresh meat would be nice to have for supper tonight."

Jessie took her time about doing things after Frank James and Ki left the following morning. She bathed leisurely in the small pond, dipping water from it in her cupped palms with which to wash and rinse. She walked idly around, naked, letting the faint breeze dry her body before she put on her clothing.

She ate a cold lunch at noon, and lay on her bedroll for a half-hour. Then, unaccustomed as she was to having nothing to do, she picked up her rifle and saddled her livery horse. Wishing that the animal was Sun, she rode in a sweeping semicircle away from the gorge, her eyes searching the landscape for signs of antelope.

She spotted a small herd, perhaps two dozen animals, after she'd been riding a half-hour. Unused to having humans in their vicinity, the antelopes did not bolt at once. They grazed calmly, watching her as she walked her mount closer to them. Their heads began to swivel rapidly and their big ears started flapping as she drew closer; then she picked her target and triggered off a shot that dropped the young buck she'd selected.

At the report of the shot, the antelopes bolted, bouncing over the arid land, scattering as they escaped. Jessie rode up to the one she'd brought down, dismounted, and gutted it. Then she lifted the carcass and draped it across her horse's rump and rode leisurely back to camp. She'd skinned the antelope and was kneeling beside the carcass to quarter it before cutting haunch steaks from the hindquarters when Ki and Frank James returned. Leather sacks closed with thongs hung from their saddle-horns.

"Fresh meat for supper!" James said. "And breakfast, too!"

"I thought we'd enjoy some antelope steaks," Jessie replied. "They'll be a change from jerky and cheese."

"And a welcome one, too," Ki put in. "Do you want me to grill them, Jessie?"

"No, I'll do the cooking," she replied. "But if you men aren't too tired, you can pick up whatever deadwood there is in the cedars over there, and start a fire. If it's lighted now, it'll be just about burned down to coals by the time I finish cutting up this carcass."

"Sure." James nodded. "You might as well start now, Ki. As soon as I unsaddle the horses, and get the sacks off them, I'll come give you a hand."

James removed the leather sacks from Ki's horse and

dropped them beside his bedroll as Ki started toward the cedar grove. James unsaddled Ki's mount, then took the sacks of loot from his own horse and carried them to put with the others. He was bending forward to swing the heavy sacks into place when a rifle-shot broke the still air and the slug whistled above James' head. Jessie looked up when the rifle's bark sounded, and started to get to her feet.

"Stay down, Miss Jessie!" Frank James called.

He was already beside his horse, one foot in his stirrup, getting ready to swing into the saddle. Jessie dropped flat and began crawling toward her saddle-gear, where she'd left her rifle after she'd unsaddled after her hunt.

Another rifle-shot cracked in the still air. This time the slug passed an inch or so above James' shoulder and grazed his mount's rump. The horse began bucking and trying to wheel, but James yanked at the reins. The horse tried to pull away, to raise its head and rear, but the outlaw's grip on the reins was too firm. He held the animal in check until he could swing up onto its back and settle into his saddle.

Whipping his rifle from its scabbard, James let off two quick shots in the general direction from which the invisible rifleman's fire had come. Then he kicked his horse to a jumping start. Bending low over the animal's neck, he galloped away.

Jessie had reached her own rifle by now. She pulled it from the scabbard and held it ready to shoulder as she scanned the featureless landscape. She was still unsure of the spot from which the sniper's shot had come, until she saw Frank James galloping after another rider.

James was almost a quarter of a mile away when Jessie saw him. The man he was chasing had a substantial lead. Ki came up then, running from the cedar grove.

"What happened? Who was shooting at you?" he asked.

"You know as much about that as I do, Ki," she replied without taking her eyes off the riders, now almost a mile away. "But I think those shots were aimed at Frank James, because one bullet nicked his horse while he was starting to get on it. Whoever it was shooting at us missed, and"—she gestured toward the now-distant figures of James and the sniper—"you saw the rest of it, I'm sure."

"Yes, I suppose I did," Ki replied. "I was in the cedars picking up deadwood and couldn't see anything until I got into the clear. Frank James was just getting on his horse, and I don't think I've ever seen a man waste as little time as he did when he went into action."

They fell silent then, watching the two riders through the clear air of the high desert country. They saw the man in the lead twist in his saddle, a revolver in his hand. Attenuated by distance in the thin air of the high desert, the reports of his pistol were tiny pops when he fired twice in quick succession.

James did not fire back, but Jessie and Ki could see that he'd sheathed his rifle now, and had drawn his pistol. He rode bending forward in the saddle, shielding himself behind the neck of his horse. The man he was pursuing twisted in the saddle of his galloping horse and fired at James again, three shots this time. Now James returned his quarry's fire.

One puff of powdersmoke rose from James' revolver, and then, after a moment's pause, another. The second shot went home. The man in the saddle of the leading horse sagged forward on his mount's neck, then tumbled limply to the ground. The riderless horse galloped on for a short distance and stopped.

Frank James dismounted when he reached the motionless form that lay sprawled on the ground. He bent over the still figure for a moment and stood erect again. Then he remounted and toed his horse up to the fallen rider's mount. Taking the reins, he led the animals back to the body and lifted it to lie across the saddle. Then he mounted his own horse and started back toward Jessie and Ki.

"I suppose we'll find out now what all this was about," Jessie said. "I only hope that wasn't a deputy sheriff or some other kind of lawman that Frank James killed."

"I think it's more likely that the dead man was one of his own kind," Ki suggested. "Perhaps some enemy he'd made in the past."

"Well, there's nothing to be gained by standing here guessing," Jessie went on. "We'll find out soon enough."

Chapter 13

"We're both relieved that that man missed you," Jessie told Frank James as he reined up in front of her and Ki. "Did you know who he was and why he'd be shooting at us?"

James's anger showed in the sharp words that came from his tight lips, and in the set of his jaw as he glanced over his shoulder at the limp form of the dead man lying across the horse he'd been riding. With an effort that was almost visible, he controlled his anger and swung out of his saddle.

"Of course I know," he replied to Jessie's question. "But he didn't have any grudge against you and Ki, Miss Jessie. It was me he was after, and I'm right sorry I put you and Ki in the danger of taking a bullet that wasn't meant for you. I hoped we'd get our job done without running into trouble of this kind."

"I've been shot at before," Jessie told him calmly. "And I can't blame you for what someone else did."

"Well, that's a real nice way to take it," James said, relief showing in his usually impassive face. "But I hope it won't happen again."

"We'll just have to be a little more careful," Jessie said.

Then she went on: "You said you knew the dead man. Not that it's any of my business, but who was he?"

"Jack Keen was his name," James told her. "He used to ride with Big Nose George Parrot's gang. A few years back, when Dingus wanted to stay with Zelda while she was waiting for their baby to be born, I joined up with Big Nose's outfit for two or three jobs. Keen was one of the gang, and we didn't exactly hit it off. We never did get to the name-calling point, much less drawing against each other, but we didn't stand up at the bar next to one another, either."

"Then why would he follow us here and try to kill us?" Jessie frowned. "Are you sure he didn't dislike you more than you realized at the time?"

James shook his head. "No, I knew from the start that we just wouldn't hit it off together. I had a name, and he didn't, and I could see it galled him. But it's easy to figure out why he jumped us. The Pinkertons have put up a big reward for Dingus and me. I told you that from the start; I didn't try to lie to you."

"Yes, I understand that." She nodded.

"I think I said there's a lot more reward money on us than the ten thousand Allan Pinkerton's offered, and everybody that's put out a poster promises they'll pay off whether we're dead or alive. Keen must've seen us get off the train at Rock Springs, or maybe he spotted me even before that. He decided he'd try for that reward money, so he trailed us."

"And decided it would be safer to bring you in dead," Ki said when James paused.

"That's about the size of it, Ki." James nodded. "But he knew Dingus and me had a lot of loot cached away. He might've figured I was setting out to dig up some of it, and

143

had it in mind to dog along after me and get the reward money and what I'd dug up as well."

"I don't suppose we'll ever know why he followed us, now that he's dead," Jessie said thoughtfully.

James shook his head. "Not likely, Miss Jessie. But if Ki feels like giving me a hand, we'll bury him. I wouldn't leave the dirtiest dead dog to be chewed up by coyotes out here on this bare prairie."

"I don't mind helping you," Ki replied. "I'll get the shovel and we'll dig him a grave. Do you have a shovel or anything to dig a grave with?"

"We don't need to do that, Ki," James said. "There's a lot of little rifts in the ground along the gorge. We'll lower him into the first one that fits, and pile rocks on him. We've got time to do that much before dark."

"This is the third place you and your brother own that we've been to," Jessie said to Frank James after he'd pointed out the distant structures that marked the horse ranch. They were like dollhouses in the distance, huddled into a sheltered saucerlike basin that made a huge dimple in the rolling prairie. "It's not really any of my business, but are there some others we haven't visited yet?"

"Oh, we've got a little bit more property scattered here and there," he answered. "Mostly houses in towns where we've tried to settle down. And we've got a farm or two that're sharecropped. We've made sure we won't be without a place to settle down in when we give up the owl-hoot trail."

"You really are going to give it up, then?" she asked.

"I might be a lot of things, Miss Jessie, but I'm not any kind of liar," James told her. "Just like I promised you, if you can get the political muckety-mucks to give Dingus

144

and me some reasonable time in jail, so's we won't be real old men when we get out, we'll quit in a minute."

"They just might be impressed enough by the amount of loot you're offering to return to listen to you," Ki put in. "I've noticed that money seems to talk louder to politicians than it does to most others."

Jessie had been studying the buildings ahead of them while they rode. She said now, "Tell me about the horse ranch, Mr. James. How did you happen to buy it?"

"We didn't buy it, Miss Jessie; we started it. There wasn't anything but bare range here when we bought this land. You see, Dingus and me were hiding out up here quite a while ago. We were wanted for a train holdup we'd pulled, and had to go all the way to Uncle Jack's Indian Camp on the Green River to find a safe hideout. That's where we ran into a real fine horse-trainer. He's a black man, and his name's John Trammell, but everybody just calls him Nigger John."

"So you took the money from the train robbery and bought the land for your horse farm?" Ki asked.

"Well, it wasn't exactly that way, but we had some money between us, so we got the idea it'd be a good thing for us to start a horse farm," James said. He turned to Jessie. "I guess you and Ki both know how it is to buy horses; you have quite a lot of them on the Circle Star."

"Of course we do," Jessie replied. "My father had the idea of breeding some, but it never did work out. There were always too many jobs to do. Sun is the only horse that he bought for breeding stock, and when I admired him so much, Alex gave him to me. Then—well, I guess you know that Alex was murdered and I had to take over the ranch as well as his other businesses. Horse-breeding just didn't fit in."

James nodded. "There's a mite of difference, though.

145

I'll agree with you, Miss Jessie—you need good horse-flesh on a ranch. But when you're outlawing, you've got to have the very best there is. Even the best ones don't last long, the way we have to ride sometimes. Well, Nigger John's the best horse-trainer I ever saw work. So, we set him up in business."

"And when you need a new horse, you simply come up here and get one." Jessie nodded. "Just like we buy them from dealers when we need more for the hands."

"Oh, there's more to it than that," James said. "And I don't guess I'd be giving anything away if I told you and Ki. We've got horses all over everywhere. We've got friends who keep some of them for us, and we board some at livery stables here and there. Nigger John sees to that, too."

"I understand now why you bought that place down on the Canadian," Jessie told him. "My father was interested in horse-breeding, among other things, so I understand that you have to start with good stock if you expect to breed good riding horses."

Frank James nodded. "That's about the size of it. We had a run of scrubs a while back, and Nigger John told us we ought to be sending him better stock, so we decided to start breeding some."

Her voice thoughtful, Jessie remarked, "You know, Mr. James, if you'd put your talent into some kind of—of, well, activity, you'd be a very successful businessman today."

He nodded. "Maybe so. Maybe if I hadn't grown up when the war was just breaking out, and if Dingus and I hadn't joined up with Quantrill, and got used to the kind of life we led with him, things could've been different. But it didn't happen that way, so I don't waste much time thinking along those lines."

146

They fell silent. By now they were close enough to the horse-ranch to make out its details, and Jessie studied its layout. A four-strand barbwire fence ran across the front, both ends of it extending to the horizon. A square extension of the fence enclosed two houses—one large, the other small and compact—as well as the three barns and four small pole-corrals that formed the core of the establishment.

There were three or four horses in the inner corrals, and beyond, within the fenced range, there were a dozen or so other horses grazing. A sizeable creek ran outside the fence on the west side, its water diverted by ditches to run close to the barns and between the corrals. Two or three men were visible, in the corrals and by the barn.

Frank James broke in on Jessie's examination. He said, "I guess there's one or two things I'd better tell you and Ki before we get to the house. Up here, folks know me under the name of B. J. Woodson, and all they know about me is that I've got a farm back in Missouri. Jesse's name here is Bob Howard, but I'd just as soon we don't talk about him."

"Doesn't anybody, even John Trammell, know who you really are?" Jessie frowned, her brows pulled down.

"Oh, John knows, but he won't let on. We go way back with old John, to when the war was just over. Dingus and me tried our hand at gathering wild horses and driving them south, where everybody needed farm stock. That's where we met Nigger John. He had a little stable up by old Fort Casper and we set him to rough-breaking the wild horses we'd round up."

"How long will it take us to clear out the stashes you have in this part of the country?" Jessie asked.

"Let's see, now," James said thoughtfully. "The furthest one's on the Lodgepole, just below where it flows into the North Platte. Then there's one on Beaver Creek up by the Wind River reservation. And the other two are along the

Powder River. One's right alongside the river and the other one's a little way below Crazy Woman Creek."

"That's going to take a lot of riding," Ki commented.

"Not so much, Ki," James said quickly. "On the train, we'll be able to get within a short day's ride to all of those stashes."

Turning to Jessie, Ki said, "If you'd like for me to, Jessie, I can go with Mr. James from the railroad, and you can stay behind and rest."

"Thank you, Ki," Jessie replied. "But I'd just as soon go along. When the time comes, I want to be able to say that I saw with my own eyes what came out of those hidey-holes when they were opened. That's why I came along, you know." Turning to James, she went on: "But I would enjoy resting a few days here at your horse ranch before we start out again."

"Why, sure, Miss Jessie," James answered. "We're all ready to stop a little while and not have anything to do except lazy around. Now it looks like Nigger John's spotted us, because here he comes to open up the gate."

As John Trammell came closer, Jessie could see that he was not a full-blood black man, but a mulatto—perhaps a quadroon. His features were sharp and aquiline, and gave no clue as to his age, though she decided from the way he moved that he could not be more than forty. He waved at Frank James and made a small bobbing bow in the direction of Jessie and Ki.

"Glad you've come for a visit, Mr. Woodson," he called as he came within easy talking distance of the fence. His speech was that of an educated man. "It's been a long time since you were here last."

"Longer than I like, John," James said. "And we'll be staying awhile this time. I hope there's nobody in the little

148

house, because I want this lady here to have it all to herself."

"We've got three buyers here, but they're in the main house," Trammell answered as he swung the gate open. "And two of them have already finished their trading; they'll be gone before supper. I can send the other one with them, if you'd rather not have him stay."

"There's no reason to do that," James said. "Nobody's ever tumbled to me before, and they might get suspicious if you asked somebody to leave before they finish their business. No, we'll make do, John. You've got plenty of room."

"Sure." Trammell nodded. "Where will you and . . ." He looked at Jessie and Ki with a frown, as though he was puzzled at Frank James's choice of companions, then went on: "Where will you all want to stay, in the big house or the little one?"

"Oh, we'll be splitting up," James replied. "This gentleman is Ki. He works for the lady. Her name is Miss Starbuck. Ki'll be staying in the main house, and so will I. Miss Jessie will have to have the little house all to herself."

"It's ready for her to move in," Trammell said. "And I'll see that everything's taken care of."

"I know you will," James replied. "We'll ride on up there now and unload; then we'll rest until suppertime."

When Jessie entered the big house after a washtub bath and a restful nap, she was surprised to see three familiar faces instead of the two she'd expected. Standing beside Ki was Paul Lawson, one of the several horse-brokers who visited the Circle Star at regular intervals.

"Jessie Starbuck!" Lawson exclaimed when she came into the room.

"Why, Paul!" Jessie smiled. "I had no idea you were one of Mr. Trammell's customers."

Lawson stepped up to greet her, his handsome bronzed face breaking into a smile as she looked up to meet his twinkling blue eyes. He stood a half-head taller than Jessie, and in their past business meetings she'd found him to be honest, forthright, and courteous. He was perhaps four or five years older than Jessie, and she'd learned during their business meetings at the Circle Star that he was unmarried.

Lawson said, "Ki told me that you were here, and I've been looking forward to seeing you again. I suppose it's Mr. Woodson who's been praising John's horses to you?"

"He's told me about them." Jessie nodded. Then, to keep Lawson from asking questions, she added quickly, "But I really didn't come here to buy horses, Paul. Ki and I just happened to be in the neighborhood and rode up with Mr. Woodson for a visit."

"Well, John Trammell's horses are as fine as any breeder I know of," Lawson said. He turned to Ki and asked, "You'd agree with me, I'm sure, Ki."

"Oh, yes." Ki nodded. "The few we saw when we were coming up to the house looked very good indeed."

Lawson said, "I haven't mentioned him to you because there are so many other horse-ranches closer to the Circle Star. But I've been dealing with John for quite a few years now. If you're interested in his horses, I certainly won't try to change your mind, even if it means losing you as a customer."

"Don't worry about that," Jessie told him. "And don't stop calling on the Circle Star. We'll still need the usual number of working horses."

"I'm glad to hear that," Lawson said, nodding. "And I hope you'll give me the pleasure of sitting by me at supper."

"Why, of course," Jessie said. "I'm sure neither Ki nor Mr. Woodson will mind, since we've been in each others' company on the way up here."

Trammell came in just then and called the group to supper. Like the meals on most of the ranches with which Jessie was familiar, the meal was eaten in businesslike fashion, with very little conversation. As they stood up from the table, Lawson turned to Jessie.

"It's still daylight," he said. "Would you like to stretch your legs after a day in the saddle? Perhaps we could walk down to the corrals and take a look at Trammell's horses."

"Why—I think I'd like that," Jessie replied, hiding her surprise. "I really didn't get a chance to look at the horses when we rode in. We were so saddle-cramped that we weren't interested in anything but washing off the trail-dust."

Jessie and Lawson strolled leisurely across the barren, hoof-pocked ground near the house and on to the corrals. Now that they were alone, Lawson was less chatty than he'd been at first. For the first time since their chance encounter, he seemed a bit ill at ease.

Reaching the first of the four small corrals, they looked at the horses inside. It was obvious to Jessie's expert eyes that they were wild, just captured from one of the herds that were commonplace on the lonelier plateaus of Wyoming Territory. The animals grew skittish as Jessie and Lawson reached the corral bars and stopped to look at them.

"They'll make good enough workhorses, but they're just everyday stock," Lawson remarked. He pointed to the horses' rough, matted coats and unshod hooves and wild-glaring eyes. "They're still spooked from fighting the lead-rope. I don't think even Trammell can make much of them."

151

"I'd want better mounts than they'll make, if I was buying for the Circle Star," Jessie commented. "Let's see what's in the other pens."

They walked around the corner of the small corral. The shallow stream that flowed along the fence had eaten away the edges of the bed and left a strip of earth only five or six inches wide between its surface and the bottom fence-rail, and Jessie turned to face the corral as she held on to the top corral rail and inched along the soggy ground. The big paint stallion that was in the corral alone nickered and pranced skittishly at their approach.

"He's as wild as a panther," Lawson said. "Even Trammell's going to have his hands full when he starts breaking this one."

"He's spooked right now," Jessie replied, taking her eyes off the thin strip of earth she was sidling along. "He'll be—"

Her words ended in a surprised gasp as the ground gave way under her feet. She threw herself forward, trying to regain her balance, but lost her grip on the rail. Twisting, she tried to take another step, but the ground was too slippery. She fell, and her frantic gyrations pushed her forward and threw her between the top and bottom rails. Her head and upper torso shot into the corral, her waist and hips balancing on the bottom fence-rail.

"Hold on, Jessie!" Lawson said as he started toward her. "I'll help you up."

Before Jessie could reply, the thudding of the paint stallion's hooves sounded. He spanned the width of the small enclosure in two leaps and reared up on his hind legs, his iron-hard front hooves flailing and ready to strike.

Chapter 14

When Lawson saw the stallion rearing up he knew he had no time to waste. Instead of trying to pull Jessie free he thrust his head and shoulders between the corral bars, shielding her body with his own.

His sudden move startled the rearing horse. It tried unsuccessfully to back away and escape from the strange object that had appeared so suddenly, but its full weight was now on its hind legs and the stallion could not move freely. It held its forequarters high, its front hooves churning, an unaccustomed posture which was beginning to throw the big steed off balance.

For a moment the horse tottered as its front legs flailed the air. Then its own efforts to maneuver pulled it down. But its attempt to back away had changed its position. The stallion's forefeet churned for a moment in midair before they descended and the hooves that would have landed squarely on Lawson's back merely grazed one of his shoulders.

Spooked by the totally foreign experience it had just undergone, the stallion wasted no time in getting away. Snorting and tossing its head, it trotted to the opposite side of the corral.

Lawson did not move until Jessie's movements as she

tried to slip to one side of his close-pressed body brought him back to the reality of the moment. He groped for the corral rail and levered himself to his feet, then extended his hand to Jessie and helped her stand up.

As his arm took Jessie's weight, the sudden pulling on the bruised muscles where the paint's hoof had landed caused Lawson to wince. After she'd gotten her balance on the slippery strip of ground, she looked at him, frowning.

"Your arm's injured," she said.

"It doesn't hurt much," he replied. "I'm all right."

"Nobody's all right who's just been hit by a horse's hoof," Jessie told him. "And it's my fault for being so clumsy and careless."

"Well, my shoulder is just a little bit sore," Lawson admitted. "But I've been hurt a lot worse."

"Just the same, it needs attention. We're going up to the house I'm staying in right this minute. I have a bottle of arnica in my saddlebags; that'll ease the pain and keep it from getting worse. Now, don't argue, Paul. Just come along."

They covered the short distance to the little house in silence. The sky was darkening now; it was the deeper blue that appeared between sunset and darkness. Inside the house, it was too dark to see well, and Jessie lighted the lamp. She went to her saddlebags and found the bottle of liniment. When she turned to take a towel from the washstand and saw Lawson standing watching her, she frowned.

"You'll have to take off your vest and shirt," she said. "If your arm's too sore, I'll help you."

Lawson started to slide out of his vest, but when he moved his arm the pain in his shoulder brought a grimace of pain to his face.

"Sit down on the bed," Jessie commanded. "And just keep still while I attend to that shoulder."

Stepping to the bed, Jessie slid Lawson's vest off. Then

154

she unbuttoned his shirt and took it off as well, moving slowly and carefully to avoid straining his injured shoulder. When she saw the angry, red palm-sized blotch on his skin, she shook her head, then filled her cupped palm with the liniment and began rubbing it gently over the reddened area.

"That's already beginning to take the pain away," Lawson told Jessie after she'd been massaging his shoulder for several minutes. He had twisted to look up in her face, and there was no way for her to misread the message that was in his eyes. He went on: "It's feeling pretty good now. If you don't mind rubbing my shoulder for just a little while longer, I'm sure it'll be all right."

Jessie continued her slow massaging. The gentle friction of her palm over Lawson's skin was beginning to bring fresh thoughts to her. She was recalling the words of the wise old geisha to whom Alex Starbuck had entrusted a much younger Jessie to be taught the private ways of men and women.

"If a man you have not known before begins to attract you, do not wait for him to ask you to bed with him," her teacher had told her more than once. *"Think quickly at such times, and do not be too timid to ask him yourself, for fear that he will disappoint you. Perhaps he is one who will bring you feelings you have never had before. There is but one way to discover which path he will lead you on, and that is to accept him the first time. If you are disappointed, and he invites you to bed a second time, you can always refuse him."*

Looking at Paul Lawson, his biceps slack now, but still bulging with latent strength, his smooth, clear skin warming the palm of her hand as she rubbed the liniment over his shoulder, Jessie made her decision quickly.

Leaning further forward, she pressed her lips against Paul Lawson's uninjured shoulder and moved them lightly along the cord of muscle that ran from the base of his neck to the shoulder's end. Lawson gave a start, and she could

155

feel the cord of muscle grow taut. Then she reversed the path her lips had taken, but this time with the warm moist tip of her tongue protruding.

"What on earth are you doing, Jessie?" he asked.

"Don't pretend that you haven't had enough experience to know," she whispered softly.

"Oh, I know well enough," he replied. "But I can't quite believe it."

"Why not?" she asked, running her fingers through the matted brush that curled on his chest.

"Because you—well, because you've always seemed a bit distant when I've seen you at the Circle Star."

"We're hundreds of miles from there now."

"But you and Ki—"

"Ki was my father's friend and helper, Paul. He's also mine. That's all."

"Then, you won't object—" he began.

Jessie broke in. "If I was going to object, I'd be handing you back your shirt right now." She moved over to the table and blew out the lamp and said, "Now we won't be interrupted."

"No," Lawson agreed. "From what I've seen when I've been here before, John will keep the others talking horses until they're sleepy enough to go to bed. But won't Ki and Mr. Woodson wonder where we've disappeared to? I wouldn't want your reputation to suffer, Jessie."

"It won't," she assured him. "I don't know Mr. Woodson very well, but he seems to be somewhat close-mouthed, and Ki never questions what I do in my personal life."

By this time Jessie had returned to stand beside the bed. Her eyes were beginning to adjust to the darkness now, and she could see Lawson as a dim ghostly shape in the gloom.

"Do you feel all right now?" she asked.

"What you've just said has made me feel better than the

156

liniment did, Jessie!" he exclaimed. Standing up, he moved to embrace her, and Jessie lifted her face to let him find her lips.

While they kissed, Lawson brushed Jessie's low-necked blouse over her soft shoulders. She shrugged her arms free and stood quietly for a few moments while he bent to caress her swelling breasts. As Lawson's lips and tongue found her budded tips, Jessie levered out of her boots and busied her fingers with the buckle of his belt. Feeling the warmth of her hands, Lawson broke their kiss and fumbled at the waist of her skirt until he found and freed the buttons of its waistband.

When Jessie felt her skirt and petticoat slipping down her hips she busied her fingers with the buckle of Lawson's belt, and pushed his trousers and balbriggans down. Her soft hand closed around his rigid shaft, and she grasped it and sank back, letting herself fall to the bed, pulling Lawson with her. He kneeled on the bed above her, and when Jessie spread her thighs and guided him he thrust at once, filling her, while she clasped her legs around his hips to pull him deeper.

Lawson began stroking, and Jessie met his lusty thrusts with a quickening rhythm. Small, gasping sighs began pulsing from her throat. Her sighs grew louder as she approached the threshold where unendurable pleasure at last became fulfillment. Then she crossed that threshold with small cries of ecstasy, while her partner joined her in a final shuddering spasm.

They lay quietly then, until Lawson raised himself on one elbow and glanced down through the gloom at Jessie's face. "I'm glad that stallion cut up the way it did," he told her. "If it hadn't been for that, I don't think I'd've had the nerve to talk about anything but horses. And I sure hate to get up and leave, but there's—"

Jessie broke in. "There's nothing right now but the rest of the night," she said. "Even if we can't make it last as long as we'd like, we can make the most of what we have while we're here together."

"It's too bad we're going to have to do such a lot of back-tracking and willywawing around, Miss Jessie," Frank James said as the engine whistled and the train began to slow down for its next stop at Casper. "But it'll all come out right, I guess."

"I'm sure it will," Jessie agreed. "And it just makes good sense to clear out the two sites up in the Powder River country first, before we go down to the Lodgepole."

"Backtracking will even save us time in the end," Ki said. He was sitting in the seat in front of Frank and Jessie, facing them. At Cheyenne, where they'd changed trains from the Southern Pacific to the Burlington Line for the final leg of their trip to Casper, they'd found that the passenger coach they'd boarded was one of the new kind in which the seats could be reversed. The arrangement formed a sort of open compartment which allowed the three of them to travel in a more companionable fashion.

Ki went on: "It's not really any of my business, Mr. James, but I'm curious. Do you mind telling us why you have two stashes as close together as the ones we're heading for now?"

"Why, that's not any secret, Ki," James replied. "But I guess if you come down to it, Dingus and I don't have many secrets left anymore."

"Anything you've already told Ki and me about your hiding-places will keep on being between the three of us," Jessie put in quickly. "And so will anything else you tell us."

"Oh, I know that, Miss Jessie," James assured her. "It just never did cross my mind that I didn't have time to explain all the things we had to do when we were running from the Pinkertons. When they got hot on our trail after we'd held up a train over in Dakota Territory we headed west, like we generally did. Well, we'd made a good haul, and our saddlebags were loaded."

When James stopped for breath, Jessie said, "I don't think you need to bother with all the details, Mr. James. You've told Ki and me so much already that I'm beginning to think of the danger you'd be in if we made a slip of the tongue."

"Now, that stopped bothering me a long time ago," James said. "You've been as patient as a saint with me, Miss Jessie. Now, Ki, the reason we've got two stashes close together is a real simple one. Our horses were tired, and after we'd crossed the Belle Fourche we decided we'd better stop and hide away part of what we were carrying. We hit the Powder River and found a place and buried half of the gold, but we hadn't much more than started out again before we saw we hadn't unloaded enough. So we made another stop on Crazy Woman Creek and buried the rest. Then we rode on into Casper and holed up."

Ki nodded. Then he said, "Jessie and I learned a little about the Powder River country some time ago. We had a brush with some outlaws and rustlers who were trying to take over the spread of a rancher who'd been the foreman of the Circle Star."

"And we were very glad to get back to Texas after we'd done what we could up here," Jessie added as the train came to a stop at the Casper depot. "But it'll be interesting to see the country again."

"We don't have much further to go, Miss Jessie," Frank James said as they reined in to rest their horses. "But I guess you know that, since you and Ki have been up in this Powder River country before."

They were riding fresh mounts that they'd gotten at the horse ranch, and they led a pack-horse with their provisions and bedrolls on it. Though the animals had shown no signs of tiring, James had stopped them halfway up a long, sloping rise, with another four or five miles of rising ground still ahead.

"We're quite a way beyond the area that Ki and I got acquainted with," Jessie replied. "It lies to the west and south."

"Well, we'll get to the creek after we top this rise we're on now," James went on. "And all we've got to do then is ride along by the creek until we hit the spot where Dingus and I put our stash. Then it's just a little hop-skip-and-jump east to the Powder River. After that, we'll be riding down-hill to the Lodgepole, and that'll do us for this time."

"We must be getting close to the end of our trip," Ki said as they started the horses moving again.

"Just about," James nodded. "After we clear up the one on the Lodgepole we've only got two more. They're way to the east and south of here, and both of them are easy to get to."

They rode on in silence, up the long slope and across two or three creek beds. None of the trickling threads of water in the sandy-bottomed courses was wider than a hand-span in width, or more than the length of a finger in depth. As they topped the slope, the ground dropped away abruptly to the west, and what had been a horizon as level as though it had been sliced by a knife-blade, was replaced by the jagged crests of mountains. A short distance ahead, the ground was broken by a winding valley.

"I'm glad we're not going to have those to cross," Jessie commented.

"We'll be heading for that little break just ahead of us," James told her, pointing to the valley. "It's kind of a pass down to the creek we're heading for. We're just about there, so the horses won't be straining too much."

On the downslope to the creek they made faster progress. The sun was not yet at noon before they reached the stream and turned to follow it in its lazy downward course. Frank James did not suggest that they stop at noon, but kept pushing ahead, and Jessie and Ki had no option but to follow him.

In the early hours of the afternoon, James pointed ahead. "There's where we're headed. That rock outcrop over the creek is where we'll pull up."

Jessie and Ki looked ahead. They'd ridden along the thread-thin trail to which Frank James had led them beyond the pass until it forked at the shallow creek they were now following. "This is the one the local folks call Crazy Woman Creek," he said as they dismounted to drink from the small clear stream before bringing their horses up to water them. After the horses had been allowed to drink and they were getting ready to mount once more, Frank James pointed to the northern fork of the trail.

"We'll hit the first cache just a little ways upstream along this branch," he said, "where it runs into the Powder River. The other one's not too far, either. It's a real short ride to the Powder, where the loot's tucked away. We ought to get to it while there's still plenty of daylight left to empty it out."

"And you mentioned that the one on the Lodgepole is the last one in Wyoming Territory," Jessie said. "Where will we be heading after it's emptied?"

"After that we'll be going to what Dingus and I call our own home grounds, Miss Jessie," Frank James replied. "Back east to Missouri. We'll need to talk with Dingus and get a count of how much cash we're gong to turn in before you call on the governor and tell him we're ready to hang our guns up and surrender if he gives us any kind of a reasonable deal."

"I've already promised that I'll do the best I can for you

and your brother," Jessie said. "And that's exactly what I intend to do."

James nodded and turned his attention back to studying the banks of the little stream. They'd traveled on less than an hour when he reined in and swung to the ground.

"This is where we've been heading for," he said. "You don't even need to get off your horses unless you feel like stretching your legs again. It'll only take me a minute to get to that bag of gold."

At the point where they'd stopped, the creek was only a few inches deep. Its crystalline water flowed over a rocky bottom, a shelf of the jagged, cracked formation of schist that rose on the opposite side of the creek to form its bank. The creamy stone rose in a rough crack-seamed wall to the height of James' head as he waded into the inches-deep water and splashed across the creek in two long steps. He walked upstream a few paces, studying the rock wall.

Jessie and Ki dismounted and followed him, walking parallel to his course on the opposite side of the stream. They stopped when James did. He'd halted in front of a wide crack that was jammed with crumbling rock from the formation. They watched as he pulled out the loose rocks, most of which were small, irregularly shaped pebbles only a couple of inches in diameter.

He'd tossed away enough of the broken bits of stone to open the wide crack halfway to the water's edge when he gave a grunt of satisfaction and plunged his hand into the crack. It was obvious that what he'd uncovered inside was heavy, for he had to insert his free hand into the crevasse to lift out a leather bag, which he held up for Jessie and Ki to look at. The bag was twice the size of a man's head, and its dark sides were crusted with dust to which a few small splinters of the whitish rock were still clinging. In spite of the dust, Jessie and Ki could read the U.S. MINT stencil and the figures $20,000 on the bag.

"Here we are," he announced. Still holding up the bag, he stepped back across the creek and lowered it to the ground beside Jessie and Ki. "Just as good as when we stowed it away."

"How long ago was that?" Ki asked.

"Let's see." James frowned. "Going on three years now. We held up that train in June. When the conductor opened the safe in the baggage coach, there were three of these bags tagged to go to a bank up in Sheridan. We'd stopped the train over close to Belle Fourche, and Dingus and the boys and me stopped after we'd covered about ten miles. We split one of the bags between Red Monkus and Joe Mancuse, and took the other two with us. Then we hid that one I told you about over east on the Powder River and stopped here to ditch this one when it got to us how much it was going to slow down our getaway."

"Then the next place we'll stop is at the place where you hid the other bag?" Jessie asked.

"That's right, Miss Jessie. And if we start right away we can get there while there's still some daylight left. So if you and Ki are ready, let's mount up and ride."

Chapter 15

Before the Powder River came in sight, the bottom of the sun's glowing disk had dropped behind the jagged peaks of the Big Horn Mountains, but it was still high enough to cast long shadows of the trio and their horses, and the sky was still daylight-bright.

Jessie and Ki followed Frank James as he splashed his horse across the shallow river's sandy bottom and turned upstream on the opposite bank. There was no trail beside the river, nor did its sandy bottom bear any signs of a commonly-used crossing. The stream was glass-clear and was less than a foot deep, and it seemed to Jessie that each grain of sand stood out in sharp relief as its current roiled in the pocks left by their horses' hooves.

James led them beside the river for a half-mile before they saw any signs of vegetation other than a few spindly scrub cedars along the margin of the stream. Then they could see the green tops of trees breaking the blue sky ahead, and a short time later the entire stand of lodgepole pines became visible, their bare bark-mottled boles rising high above the river's sandy bank.

"There's where we're heading," James told them, nodding toward the pine trees. "And those trees look just the same as they did when Dingus and I stopped to rest our horses in what little shade they gave us."

A quarter of an hour after sighting the clump of lodgepoles, they reached the grove. Frank James guided his horse in and around between the trees, peering upward as he rode. He reined in beside the bole of a tree near the center of the stand. The top of the tree had been shattered by a lightning-bolt during some long-past storm. The lightning had cut off its branched top, and a charred line as wide as a man's hand marked the path its searing force had followed to the ground.

"A man couldn't ask for a better mark than this to show where he'd made a cache," James said, pointing to the black scar left by the lightning-bolt.

He swung out of his saddle, and while Jessie and Ki were dismounting, he walked over to the packhorse and freed the prospector's spade that was lashed to one of the panniers. Carrying the spade he went to the stunted tree and backed up to it, his shoulders centered on the charred mark left by the lightning-bolt. With carefully measured steps, James began walking away from the tree.

After a dozen paces or so—neither Jessie nor Ki had been counting—he stopped and took three sidewise steps, then began digging. The sharp, pointed blade of the short-handled space took out big bites from the crusted soil of the pine-stand, and soon James had made an excavation the size of a large bucket. He dug less vigorously now, and as he continued shoveling a frown began forming on his face. After he'd lifted out perhaps a dozen more shovelsful of the light yellow soil he stopped and shook his head.

"Something's wrong here," he said, as much to himself as to his companions. "Dingus was doing the digging here, but I kept an eye on him most of the time, and I'll take a

Bible oath that he didn't put down a hole any deeper than this one is."

"Are you sure you're digging in the right place?" Jessie asked.

"Certain-sure, Miss Jessie. Fourteen steps from whatever mark we used on the tree, because it was the fourteenth day of the month when we held up that train. You see, we'd always remember the day we pulled a job, because we'd have somebody who'd stand up in court and swear we were with them that day if the law caught up with us and we had to stand trial."

Jessie frowned. "But you paced off the distance and then moved to one side a few feet."

"That's right. We'd always take those three steps off the line so that anybody who spotted our line-mark and figured out what it meant couldn't just dig a trench along it and find what we'd buried. Then we'd dig our hole half as deep as the handle of the shovel was long. That's the way we always kept track of where we'd buried something and how deep a hole we made."

"Are you sure the handle of the shovel you've got is the same length as the one you used to dig with before?" Ki frowned.

"Ki, I've used plenty of these prospector's shovels in my day," James replied. "They're all just alike, give or take maybe an inch."

"And you're certain about the distance from the tree and the three steps to one side?" Jessie insisted.

James shook his head and said, "Now, I wouldn't be likely to forget those figures, Miss Jessie. Why, Dingus and me used them I don't know how many times, and for a lot of years. The way I see it, there's just one thing that happened to that bagful of double-eagles. Somebody watched us while we buried it, or they were trailing us and came across where we'd dug the hole while the dirt we'd filled it with was still fresh."

"That would account for it," she agreed. "But would they steal from you, Mr. James? I mean—" She stopped short when she realized that what she'd been intending to say might be a bit embarrassing both to her and to Frank James.

"What you started to ask me was would one thief steal from another thief," James said. His voice was as level of expression as it always became when he was recounting the outlaw activities of himself and his more notorious brother.

"Yes, it was," Jessie admitted.

"You can forget that old saying about there being honor among thieves, Miss Starbuck," James went on. "There's not any. Nobody knows it better than Dingus and me. We've had men in our line lie to us and try to rob us, and we've had some turn us in to the Pinkertons when they figured they might get some of the reward money that's posted on us."

"Greed counts more than honor, then?" Ki asked.

James nodded. "It sure does, Ki. So if you want my guess, the ones who took the loot we had cached was Red Monkus or Joe Mancuse, or maybe both of them. When we split away from them after that train holdup, it wouldn't've been any trick at all for them to have circled around behind us and skulked along and watched while Dingus and me buried the bag we put here."

"I don't suppose you've seen them since?" Ki asked.

"No, Ki. And it's not likely I would anytime soon, not unless I went looking for them. They—" James stopped and shook his head, then went on: "But now that I recall, Red and Joe were with Big Nose Parrot for a while when I was in his bunch, and so was Jack Keen, the fellow who was trailing us back at the Flaming Gorge. They all knew that Dingus and me put away most of our takings."

"Do you suppose they were with that man Keen at the gorge?" Jessie asked.

James shook his head. "Not likely, Miss Jessie. But the three of them were in the gang together awhile for sure, and they might've done some swapping of what they knew about where Dingus and I might've put away our takings."

"I suppose that's as good a guess as any," Jessie agreed.

"Well, it's not all that important anymore," James went on. "We've done what we came here to do, and there's plenty of stashes left to be dug up, so we might just as well give up on this place."

"I haven't looked lately at the list you gave me, but isn't our last stop in Wyoming Territory down in the south?"

"That's right. The last big stash is on the Lodgepole River. It's too late by now to cover much ground, so maybe we'd better stay the night here. Tomorrow, we'll start back to the railroad and head for Cheyenne."

"You know, Ki, I've seen enough of this up-and-down country by now to appreciate the level prairie we have back on the Circle Star," Jessie said. "At least when we're hunting stray range cattle down there we can see them a long way off."

Since leaving Cheyenne at dawn they'd been riding with the sun in their faces over a stretch of low rolling hills. The rises were not high or especially steep, but one had followed the other in such quick and seemingly endless succession that the livery horses they'd rented in town quickly grew tired. Their progress toward the river had been slow because of the many stops needed to rest them.

Frank James was riding a short distance in advance of Jessie and Ki. He'd spurred ahead to take a look at the trail where it seemingly came to a stop at a huge slash of raw soil that showed on the flank of one of the higher hills in the dozens they'd ridden up and down since leaving Cheyenne.

"I'll agree that these hills get on my nerves a little bit, too," Ki said, nodding. "But James says we'll have them behind us by noon or a little later. He told me that after we get out of this stretch of rolling country the land flattens out, and all we have between us and the Lodgepole is level prairie."

"But not before we get through these hills," Jessie said. "And I see that Frank James has turned back, so we'd better pull up and wait for him here. I suppose he's found that we'll have to swing around that big landslide ahead."

They waited in silence until James rode up and reined in beside them. "That dirt slide up ahead is just part of what's all around up there," he told them. "My guess is they had an earthquake up in these hills and nobody knew about it."

"How could that be possible?" Jessie asked.

"It can be," Ki said. "In Japan we have many of them. Some are small and in only a small area, but some are very big indeed."

"Just to be safe, we'd better swing wide toward where we're going," James suggested. "It'll take us a mite longer to get to the Lodgepole, but it's only about ten miles ahead now, and it'll take less time to cut around that mess up ahead than to try going over that busted-up ground."

"You lead the way, then," Jessie told him. "You know the country around here better than Ki or I do. We'll be right behind you."

For the rest of the morning and a good part of the afternoon they zigzagged through the hills. Frank James rode ahead, and each time he saw signs of the earthquake in their path he signaled them to follow him as he scouted ahead. Though James had estimated the distance of the stream as a dozen miles, they'd been forced to cover half again as many. The sun was hanging low in the west before they sighted the stream, a silver thread bordered by a line of green, the green fading to a deep yellow a dozen yards beyond the water's winding course.

James reined in when the Lodgepole came in sight, and waited for Jessie and Ki to reach him. "I've figured out where we are now and how much farther we've got to go," he told them.

"That's good news," Jessie said. "Can we get to the place we're heading for before dark?"

"Not unless we cut a pretty good shuck, Miss Jessie. And I know it's been a pretty hard ride so far, so if you don't feel like pushing we can stop at the first likely spot up ahead and go on to the cache tomorrow morning."

"Let's ride as hard as we can before dark," she answered. "If we get there before the horses give out, that's a day saved. If we don't—well, we'll have tried."

"It'll be a straight-line ride, then." James nodded. "And any time you want to stop, just say the word."

He waited only long enough for Jessie to nod, then wheeled his horse and started it off at a brisk trot. For the next hour, while the sun sank out of sight below the low humpy hills, and the long prairie twilight set in, they pushed their horses without stopping.

As the growing dusk began to veil the brightness of the evening sky, the horses moved more and more reluctantly, until at last James reined in at a spot where a curve in the shallow watercourse created a small, flat pocket in the valley. Jessie and Ki halted when they reached him.

"That fool earthquake got me a little bit mixed up," he told them. "When I told you we'd be able to get to where

170

we made that big cache, I thought we were a lot farther along than we were, because most of these little dips and rises look pretty much the same."

"I suppose what you're telling us is that we're not going to be able to reach the place we're looking for before dark?" Ki asked.

"That's the way it sizes up, Ki," he replied. Turning to Jessie, he went on: "Even if these horses had wings instead of legs, they can't get us where we're heading for before dark."

"If that's the case, then let's stop right here," she suggested.

"I had that in mind when I pulled up," James said, and nodded. "There's more graze here than we're likely to find anywhere close ahead, and the ground's nice and level. A half-day's ride will get us where we're going by noon tomorrow, so we'll have plenty of time to open the cache before dark. Then we can get started early the next morning and ride the hump between this creek and the next one. That'll let us cut a straight line to Cheyenne, and make it back there in one day."

"You didn't mention that you'd had any trouble when you and your brother were hiding your loot here," Jessie said, pointing to the skeleton of a horse, and the wheels and scattered boards that were all that remained of a wagon.

"We didn't," Frank James replied as he dismounted. "That horse-skeleton and the broken-down wagon were both laying here when Dingus and I found this place."

"I'd say that's what remains of some emigrant party," Ki suggested. "I suppose the Indians caught them here."

"That's what we figured, Ki." James nodded. "And it's one reason we picked out this place to make our cache."

"I don't see any human remains, though," Jessie remarked, swinging out of her saddle. "Or any graves."

"It's not likely you would," James told her. "This used to be Ute country, Miss Jessie. Dead or alive, the redskins would've hauled whoever was in that wagon to their camp for a dance. But we figured there wasn't but the one wagon, or there'd be another horse-skeleton laying around."

While Frank James talked, he'd been uncoiling the lariat that hung from his saddle string. When it was freed he'd moved to the packsaddle and taken the spade out of its lashings. He tossed the spade down beside the skeleton, then turned the coil of rope and heaved it edgewise along the ground. It unrolled for about half its length before it lost momentum and fell over.

Turning to Ki, he went on: "If you'll take hold of that end and straighten it out, we'll throw a loop around those horse-bones and drag them away from where they're laying, Ki. When we dug our cache, we dragged the skeleton on top of the fresh dirt to keep anybody from noticing where we'd been digging."

"Well, it would've fooled me," Ki said as he took the rope and helped James to circle it around the bones. "It doesn't look like it's ever been moved."

"Well, we were real careful when we shifted it," James told him. "And we fixed it up to look like it'd been there for a long time—which I had, I guess, since the last emigrants moved west before the railroads were built this far."

Both Ki and James kept working while they talked, and the horse-skeleton was soon enmeshed in a criss-cross of rope. Ki took one end of the lariat, Frank James the other, and they began to drag the skeleton out of the earth into which the action of wind and weather had partially embedded it.

As the horse-skeleton moved, its spine began to bulge just behind the ribcage. Seeing that it was in danger of snapping, Jessie hurried over and put a hand on either side of the bulge. With the men pulling and Jessie pushing, the bones slowly came out of the shallow creases that wind and weather had created. The horse-skeleton skidded slowly forward until it cleared the spot where it had been lying and rested on the untouched soil a few feet away.

"That's all we needed to do," James said. He picked up the shovel. "And we won't need to move it back. After I dig up the stuff that's buried under where it lay, I'll just fill the hole and stamp it down level again. Nobody'll ever know there was anything there."

"Why waste time filling the hole?" Jessie asked. "You'll have what was in it."

"Now, I can see you've never been an outlaw on the run, Miss Jessie," James told her. "When the law or the Pinkertons are after you, it just gets to be a habit to hide any signs that might give them a clue that you've passed that way. No, I guess I'll just fill the hole again. It won't take long, and I won't be starting any bad habits that might get me in trouble later on."

Picking up the shovel, James began tossing clods of dirt from the spot where the skeleton had lain. The earth was dry, and each stroke he made brought up a fully loaded shovel. He worked with a smooth rhythmic swing that wasted no effort and showed he'd often done similar jobs before. Only a few minutes after he'd begun tossing dirt he had an excavation three feet square and almost a foot deep to show for his efforts.

"If you'd like to rest, I'll spell you for a while," Ki offered. "With both of us working, we'll get the job done in a lot less time."

"Why, that's right nice of you, Ki." James nodded. "I sure won't tell you no."

Handing the shovel to Ki, he stepped aside. Ki began digging, his movements as efficient as James' had been. He'd deepened the hole almost another foot when the edge of the spade struck wood with a grating thunk.

"You've hit the box," James said, a smile on his usually expressionless face. "Maybe I'd better take over again and clear the rest of the dirt away."

Ki passed him the spade and James went back to work. Soon he'd exposed the entire top of a box that was roughly a yard square. Traces of black paint still clung to the boards in places where the shovel's edge had not scraped. James quickly excavated a vee at one corner of the box.

As he worked, he said, "One reason we buried this stuff here was that we could use the boards from that wrecked wagon to make this box. It took us half the day to get the job done, but we figured it was worth it."

He'd finished scooping out the slanting trench he'd dug in the ground, level to the corner of the box. Slipping the edge of the shovel under the corner board, he hit its handle with the butt of his palm, then levered the handle upward. With the small screeching of nails long in place, the top of the box tilted upward. After that, it took only a few moments for him to free the lid completely and lift it off the box.

Jessie and Ki had already stepped up to the side of the hole and were looking into it when Frank James lifted the lid and placed it beside the hole. They saw a number of canvas money-sacks and stacks of currency, most of them still bound in neat bundles that bore bank imprints.

"There must be quite a bit of money in there," Jessie said. "I suppose you'd know about how much?"

"Oh, sure, Miss Jessie," James replied. "Dingus and me

totaled it up before we closed the box. There's right at sixty thousand dollars in cash-money here, and if you add in what the jewelry in some of those sacks is worth, there'll be eighty-three thousand all told in this box here."

Although she was accustomed to dealing in large sums of money, Jessie was surprised at the figures Frank James had just mentioned. She kept her face expressionless, however.

"You and your brother have certainly been very successful bandits, Mr. James," she said. "Not that I approve of what you've done, but adding this to what we've already taken from your other hiding places, we have almost a million good reasons to use in bargaining for that pardon you and he are hoping for."

"Well, I sure hope you play your cards right, ma'am," James told her. "Because if it'll get us off the owl-hoot trail, we're ready to give up every penny of it and—"

Whatever else Frank James intended to say was lost as a rifle cracked in the distance and its lead kicked up a spurt of dirt from the heap that lined the hole.

Chapter 16

For a moment Jessie forgot the contents of the box. She dropped flat and rolled behind one of the heaps of dirt that rose beside the hole. As she moved, she drew her Colt. The dirt-pile gave her very little cover, but even a little was better than none.

At one side of her, Frank James had also flattened himself on the ground. Jessie had not seen him draw his revolver, but he had a Remington .44-.40 in his hand. His eyes were fixed on the slope across the stream, where a small stand of lodgepole pines grew near the top of the long grassy slant. Jessie glanced around, looking for Ki, but he was nowhere to be seen.

"I'm sorry this happened, Miss Jessie," James said without taking his eyes off the trees. "If my mind hadn't been so set on digging up that box, I'd've paid more attention to what was going on around us."

"I realize that you're not to blame," Jessie told him. Like James, she kept her eyes busy scanning the slope where the shot had come from. "I knew when we started that I might be taking some risks if I helped you. We've been lucky until now."

"One of the old philosophers I was reading about awhile

back said one time that luck is better than skill," James said. "I think I'd be hard put which one to take."

While James talked, Jessie scanned the landscape for Ki, but he was nowhere to be seen. She was not too surprised. Ki's *ninja* training had taught him how to become virtually invisible, even in broad daylight, and the day was now slowly fading into twilight.

Another shot rang out from the slope ahead, followed at once by its twin. Both slugs zipped over their heads, uncomfortably close.

"There are at least two of them, then," James remarked. "I suppose they've been dogging after us for quite a while; they likely picked up our trail in Cheyenne."

Before Jessie could comment another shot sounded and the whistle of a bullet cut the air between Jessie and her companion. He grunted and clasped his right shoulder.

Jessie was aware of his movements but her attention was centered on the spot from which the shot came. The instant its report had reached her ears she'd started rolling onto her back, and she leveled her Colt the instant she stopped moving.

A wisp of powdersmoke was dissipating above three or four clumps of low-growing chaparral that stood near the top of the slope. Jessie let off three quick shots, one into each of the brush-clusters, before she realized that she was wasting scarce ammunition.

No shots came from the chaparral in reply, and the smoke-thread above the bushes had almost dissipated by now. She still saw no telltale movement in the brush, but she kept her eyes fixed on it and held her fire.

"You're hit, aren't you?" she asked James.

"Not quite. Grazed," he replied calmly. "Nothing to worry about. The bullet did more damage to my coat than it did to me."

177

"Now we know there are three of them instead of two," she said calmly. "Do you have any idea who they might be?"

"I haven't got a notion to my name, Miss Jessie," James told her. "But every outlaw in the country knows that Dingus and me have a lot of money tucked away."

"And we haven't made much of an effort to hide our trail," Jessie said. "It certainly wouldn't have been much of a trick for somebody to follow us, the way that man did over at Flaming Gorge."

"You mean Jack Keen," James said. "He might've had somebody with him, at that. Even if he didn't, word travels fast on the owl-hoot trail, and we haven't been real careful about covering our tracks."

"It looks like we made a mistake, not—" Jessie's words were cut off when another shot cracked from the brush across the stream and a bullet raised another spurt of dirt from the pile of loose earth heaped in front of James. He did not fire in reply; both he and Jessie kept their eyes on the areas from which the bushwhackers were attacking.

"You were right about us making a mistake," James said. He might have been commenting on the weather. "We ought to've looked back now and then while we were traveling here. It's our own fault, but we spilt the milk, and there's no use worrying about sopping it up now."

"That's not the mistake I was thinking about," Jessie told him. "I'm thinking about our rifles. They're less than twenty feet away, but there's not a bit of cover between us and the horses."

"You've only got two shots left, if I counted right," James frowned. "But I've got a full cylinder. When I say the word, you waste one of your shots and I'll waste two of mine. We sure can't stand off those fellows without shells."

"Tell me what—" Jessie began, but let the rest of her question go unasked as Frank James barked a swift command.

"Now!" he snapped.

Almost before the word left his lips, he was firing at the lodgepole pines. He triggered his revolver so quickly that the two reports blended into one. Jessie leveled her Colt at the brush and got off the single shot James had told her to fire.

Echoes of their shots came from both the lodgepoles and the chaparral, and one slug thunked into the dirt-pile that James had been using for shelter. He was no longer there. The instant he'd loosed his lead into the lodgepoles he'd leaped to his feet and run crouching to the horses.

James freed his own rifle first. He handled the Winchester like a pistol, shooting one-handed, while his free hand groped in his saddlebag for cartridges. Dropping them into a pocket, he slid Jessie's rifle from its saddle-scabbard and started running back toward her.

Though the man on the ridge in the sagebrush did not fire, the shootists in the lodgepole stand both loosed shots. Both missed. Their lead only kicked up spurts of dirt ahead of James as he ran back to the excavation and its sheltering heaps of earth.

"Here you are, Miss Jessie," he said, handing her the gun before dropping behind the low earthen bulwark again. "I didn't take time to get you any shells, but I've got enough for both of us if we don't get wasteful."

"That was a terrible risk you took!" Jessie exclaimed.

"Not as much as it might've looked like," he replied, his eyes fixed on the lodgepole pines. "Shooting down-slope is real tricky, and none of those men who're pinning us down here have learned the trick yet.'"

Jessie heard his words but made no reply. Her attention

179

was pinned to the lodgepole pines. When the shots sounded from the trees she'd instinctively turned her head in that direction and had glimpsed the suggestion of motion at the edge of the stand. She had not seen Ki, but knew at once that it was his movement that had caught her eyes.

Before she could say anything to Frank James her intuition proved to be sound. A yell of pain burst from the trees and a man ran out of their shelter. He was clawing at his throat.

Frank James swung his rifle to cover the moving man, but Jessie closed her hand on the barrel to keep him from taking aim. "Wait," she said. "Don't waste a shell. Ki has already taken care of him."

Almost before she'd finished speaking, the running man's hands dropped from his throat and he began reeling. Even at the distance from which they were looking, Jessie and Frank James could see the gleam of the throwing-blade embedded in his throat.

"Where is Ki, anyhow?" James frowned.

"Somewhere in that stand of trees."

A shot rang out from the sagebrush on the ridge behind them. Instinct sent both Jessie and her companion diving to the ground, but like the other shots from the same hidden riflemen, this one was short. The bullet kicked up dust a yard short of them as they turned to look at the concealing bushes.

Frank James had shouldered his rifle as soon as he hit the ground. His head dropped as he sought the sights and let off two quick shots. His arm and hand were a blur of speed as he pumped the second shot into the magazine while shifting his aim.

There was no second shot from upslope, but the muzzle of a rifle slid slowly from the concealing sage. The barrel of the weapon was sagging as it came into sight, and it continued to slid downward until it hit the ground, leaving the weapon's stock leaning against the thick brush, its muzzle in the short grass at the edge of the sagebrush.

Jessie turned her attention back to the pines. She glimpsed a blur of motion between the tall, bare trunks of the lodgepoles, and had started to raise her rifle before she realized that the dark shadow might be Ki. She held her fire.

Only a few seconds ticked away before a man burst from the pine-stand. He was running down the slope, a bright gleam of the sky's dimming light reflecting from Ki's throwing-blade, which was embedded in his shoulder.

Jessie did not hesitate. The instant she saw that the running man was not Ki, she also saw that the wound from the *shuriken* would be crippling but not fatal. She brought up her rifle. Only an instant passed before she had the running outlaw in her sights, and she triggered off a shot. Her bullet finished the job Ki's blade had begun. The outlaw flung up his hands and dropped to the ground.

"You're a right smart hand with that Winchester, Miss Jessie," Frank James commented. He'd been bringing up the barrel of his own rifle when Jessie got off her shot. Now he lowered the muzzle. "I don't think there were more than those three, or they'd have been shooting, too."

She nodded. "I'm sure you're right. But we were lucky, and they were poor shots. I don't suppose you recognized either one of those we got a good look at?"

"I knew both of them, and used to ride with one of them in Doc Bender's old Powder Springs gang," James answered. "That was Joe Mancuse, the one that you brought down. The one Ki spooked out was Curly Brooks. I guess I'll know who the other one was when we go up to that sagebrush and get a look at him."

Ki came out of the lodgepoles, leading two horses. He

181

stopped to lift the lifeless forms of the outlaws, and draped them across their saddles. Then he headed toward the creek.

"I guess I'd better go up to that sagebrush and see who the other one was," James said. "And while we've still got light enough to work by, I'll dig out a little more dirt from that hole and make one grave for all three of them."

"Ki and I can start while you go up the slope," Jessie told him. "And then let's find another place to spend the night, if you don't mind."

"Whatever you say, Miss Jessie," he said, and nodded. "I can see why you'd want to camp somewhere else. When you come right down to it, outlawing can be pretty rough work sometimes."

"Can I beg a favor of you, Ki?" Frank James asked, looking across the table at him.

"Certainly." Ki nodded. "What is it?"

"I'd like to talk to Miss Jessie private-like for a few minutes," James replied. "Maybe you could visit with Joab while we're talking, or whatever else you'd fancy to do."

They were sitting at the table in the kitchen of the James boys' stud-ranch in Texas. The trip from Cheyenne had seemed an unusually tiring one, for they'd started the day after returning from the gunfight on the Lodgepole. Now, after deciding to plan their next trip after supper, Frank James' request struck Jessie as being a bit out of the ordinary, since Ki had been included in their planning from the beginning.

Jessie glanced at James when he made the unusual request. His brow was furrowed and his lips clamped tightly together as he waited for Ki's reply.

"Of course not," Ki said. He'd seen the silent signal in

Jessie's eyes and the almost imperceptible nod she'd given after hearing their companion's request. He stood up and began walking toward the door.

James watched Ki for a moment, then turned back to look at Jessie. A bit of his fading frown still showed on his face.

"I don't rightly know how to start out," he told her. "But I guess the best thing to tell you first is how much thanks I owe you—and Dingus owes you too, even if he doesn't know everything you've done for us lately."

"You don't have to thank me," Jessie said. "Or Ki, either. If we hadn't wanted to help, you'd have known about it a long time ago."

"Oh, I give you credit for being a real outspoken lady, Miss Jessie," James said quickly. "And you've held up your part of our bargain all the way. That's why I'm having such a hard time trying to say what I've had in my mind ever since that shoot-out we had with those fellows up in Wyoming Territory."

"Perhaps that will be the last trouble we'll have," Jessie suggested. "And we're getting close to the end of our job. I've been thinking about the best way to approach the authorities—actually, which ones I'll need to talk to first, and—"

"Excuse me, Miss Jessie," James broke in. "That's been bothering me a little bit, too. But that's not what's on my mind."

"Suppose you tell me what is, then."

"Well, there was a letter from Dingus waiting for me when we got here," James said. "He's in Saint Joe now, said he was getting another job ready for us, another bank."

"But you can't let him do that!" Jessie protested. "If he

or you or both of you together rob another bank, all the work we've done will be wasted!"

"Sure. I know that." Frank James nodded. "But Dingus has made a new friend while I was gone, and I guess they've been doing some scheming."

"Can you get back to Missouri in time to stop him?" Jessie asked.

"Oh, Dingus wouldn't go out on a job unless I was along," James assured her. "That's what I wanted to talk to you about. I'm going to have to cut a shuck back to Saint Joe and put the quietus on what Dingus and his new friend are cooking up. It's likely to take me a little time, and there's not any use in you and Ki sitting here waiting. I know you've got a lot of irons in the fire besides the Circle Star, and I guess all of them need some looking after."

"They do, but there's nothing urgent," Jessie said. "Are you suggesting that Ki and I go back to the ranch while you make your trip to Missouri?"

"That's about the size of it, Miss Jessie. Of course, you'd be real welcome to stay here, but you'll likely be a lot more comfortable at your own place while you're waiting."

"I'll go back to the Circle Star and wait, of course," Jessie agreed. "And Ki won't argue with my decision, if that's what's been worrying you."

"It just seems ungrateful for me to ask you to put off all the things we've been figuring on," James said. "But I'll take it as another big favor if you're agreeable."

"Ki and I can leave tomorrow," Jessie told him. "And whenever you've gotten things straightened out with your brother, we'll just pick up where we left off."

Frank James sighed with relief. "I sure appreciate it, Miss Jessie. And maybe it won't take me very long to convince Dingus that giving up, the way we planned, is the best thing to do. I'm sorta counting on this new friend he's made to help me. From what Dingus said in his letter, he's a right nice young fellow. His name's Bob Ford."

Watch for

LONE STAR AND THE MASTER OF DEATH

sixty-sixth novel in the exciting
LONE STAR
series from Jove

coming in February!